# Bad Chillies

A novel by Blair Polly

bpolly@xtra.co.nz



ISBN-13:
978-1482738391

ISBN-10:
1482738392

For my departed friends,
Mac, Rod, Graeme, Woody, and Jonathan.

# Acknowledgements

Many thanks to Barbara Polly, Sheryl Hayman, Marie Nordstrand, Suzie Belt, Frank Greenall, Ziggy Schmidt, Matt Taylor, Kate Kidman, Tapiwa Bururu, Robert MacLean Jr, Don Polly, and Anthea Whitlock for your editorial support, constructive comments, proofreading skills and general encouragement while writing this book.

Thanks to Denise McKee for her photography and cover artwork.

# CHAPTER 1 - FRIDAY AFTERNOON

When he came to, his head throbbed and the side of his face and neck felt battered. Blinking hard he tried to clear his vision, but his eyes refused to focus. He attempted to roll onto his back, but couldn't. With his face to the floor, his arms tied firmly behind his back, and his legs bound tightly together, he was helpless.

A hand grabbed his wrists raising them slightly. Then something sharp clamped onto his little finger. He wondered what was going on … but only for a moment.

As the secateurs cut through bone and tendons a searing pain flashed up his arm. He tried to scream, but tape wrapped around his lower face prevented his mouth from opening. What noise did emerge was more a grunt as the scream burned its way out his nostrils instead. In agony, with jaw clenched and eyes screwed tight, he felt his hands rise once more.

His ring finger came off with a red hot crunch, followed shortly thereafter by the middle finger. The pain was excruciating. Sweat mixed with blood ran pink onto the floor. He shook uncontrollably.

About to pass out, darkness slowly engulfing him, he felt the bite of the steel blades yet again and gritted his teeth. This time he knew what to expect. The only thing keeping him conscious now was terror.

As his index finger joined the others in a gathering pool of blood, the pain was too great, his brain switched off, and darkness took him.

Cold water thrown onto his face and head brought him back a few minutes later. As his eyelids fluttered open, he heard a mumbled voice but couldn't quite make out the words. Then his wrists began to rise once more and the secateurs went to work on the fingers of his other hand.

A morning that had held such promise had suddenly turned into a nightmare.

This would not be his lucky day after all.

# CHAPTER 2 - MONDAY MORNING

Chris Spacey, his back to the sun, and bare forearms resting on the roof of the unmarked police car, looked out at the harbour. He should have been enjoying the morning, but his imagination had other ideas. Every time he closed his eyes and tried to relax in the sun's warmth, pictures of a small fingerless hand flashed into his mind.

People assumed Chris was tough because of his size, and they were right for the most part, but tough guys have nightmares too. Recently, he'd had more than his fair share.

Chris's dark hair had a touch of grey and his olive skin tanned easily. Women found his face attractive, particularly his blue eyes. Their unusual paleness gave his gaze an intensity some people found disconcerting. When concentrating or angry, with brow furrowed, he looked aggressive and very dangerous. Even morons could tell that when it came to dealing with Chris, they would end up in a heap of pain if they made the wrong move. When he smiled however, his open face and sparkling eyes made the girls melt. He never noticed the many women that turned their heads to watch him pass.

With blond hair and grey eyes, Detective Andy Thompson, Chris's colleague, couldn't have been more different. Ten years Chris's junior, the top of Andy's head barely reached Chris's shoulder. Despite his short stature, corded muscles stood out on Andy's arms and his hands seemed those of a larger man.

Andy never stumbled when he walked over broken ground. He never tripped, he never fell. Chris thought it must have something to do with his low centre of gravity. Confident in Andy's speed and balance, Chris offered to bet his fellow detectives a week's pay that Andy could run 100 metres down the railway tracks, over the sleepers, faster than they could run it on an athletics track. So far he hadn't found any takers, which was a pity because Chris could have used the money.

Agile and quick, Andy played rugby in high school, winning most valuable player two years in a row. In his last year, he scored more points than any other halfback in the school's history. At university he swapped rugby for judo, rising steadily through the grades to gain his black belt. He even won his weight division at the national champs in Lower Hutt one year. Judo certainly helped Andy deal with the more aggressive and uncooperative people he now met on a daily basis. It rarely took him more than a second or two to subdue any suspect silly enough to throw a punch or resist arrest. A twist of a wrist, lightning-fast swivel and sidestep, would find Andy behind his opponent, in complete control. Most offenders, shocked at the speed in which they'd been immobilised, suddenly became far more cooperative.

Chris lacked Andy's finesse, but made up for it with raw power. Unfortunately for the offender, Chris's methods were considerably more painful.

Working out of Wellington Central Police Station, the pair had teamed up off and on for the last four years. They were bad influences on each other, but bad in a good way. They pushed the boundaries at times, but they also got results. Well, most of the time they got results. Occasionally they'd end up in a deep tank of shit, but both figured, that's just the way things worked out sometimes. Neither intended changing his methods. Besides, even the smell of poo washed off eventually.

The two detectives were parked up on Oriental Parade. Even at this early hour, the cafés were busy. Tables, pressed tightly together on the footpath, were full of people drinking cappuccinos, lattes and flat whites, enjoying the morning. Wellington, on a beautiful day like this, could rival any city on the planet.

Wellington's harbour, one of the world's finest natural anchorages, had only the slightest of ripples marring its mirrored surface. Beyond the harbour, cumulus clouds poked up from behind the Tararua Range to the north. To the west, the line of the city's high-rises curved around the foreshore. Even Wellington's notorious wind had gone on holiday. The February weather thus far had exceeded the forecaster's most optimistic predictions.

As Chris tried to shake the image of severed fingers out of his head, a call came through on the car's radio. Three drunks were creating a disturbance outside a bookshop in Cuba Mall.

"You going to get that?" Chris said poking his head through the window and looking at Andy sitting motionless in the passenger seat.

"Nah," Andy replied. "We've had our fair share of pissheads this week. I'll be buggered if I'm cleaning puke out of the car again."

"I'm not a big fan of puke myself. A hot coffee and something to eat has a far better ring to it."

"You're not wrong there, pal."

Ever since catching a lucky break in the Leonard Bourne case five days ago, Andy was reluctant to take routine callouts. The kudos they'd gained from solving such a high profile case had gone to Andy's head. Chris wasn't about to burst his bubble. Bubbles had a way of bursting soon enough without any help from him.

The Bourne case had been a particularly gruesome one. Parents of a young boy had paid a substantial ransom, following the kidnapper's instructions to the letter, without notifying the police. When they received a glass jar containing one of their son's fingers the following day, accompanied by a note demanding more money, the parents realised their mistake and did what they should have done in the first place. They called the police.

A courier delivered a second parcel containing a middle finger the next day and, to everyone's horror, a ring finger arrived the day after that. The kidnapper made no further contact or ransom demand. Police never even had the chance to trace a call or use their considerable forensic resources. When the fourth finger turned up, police gave up hope of further contact and realised the kidnapper was just playing with them.

Each time a parcel arrived, the distraught mother's wracking sobs filled the house. Supported by her red-eyed husband, the pair sat on the couch in the lounge feeling hopeless and helpless. Many of the detectives working the case weren't in much better shape. They had kids themselves. The situation had turned hardened cops into cry-babies.

The lack of clues made the case unusual and incredibly frustrating. Most criminals tend to be on the thick end of the intelligence scale, but on this occasion, the kidnapper had used his brain and planned well. Despite the large team and the hours of investigation, the police had little to go on. They needed a break. Fortunately for Leonard Bourne and his family, they got one.

It's funny how things work out sometimes, but Andy's love of chilli peppers proved a big help in solving the case. Jalapeños were his favourites. Much to Chris's disgust, Andy put them on almost everything he ate. He loved chillies with a passion most men reserved for women, sport, or drinking.

Toast with peanut butter and chilli for breakfast, cheese and chilli sandwiches for lunch, and anything with chilli for dinner were common. He would even snack on chillies straight from the jar. Chris tried a jalapeno once but when his mouth stopped burning, he cursed and vowed never again.

As the two detectives waited for another unit to pick up the call, Andy pulled a sandwich from a bag on the seat beside him.

"You'll never find a girlfriend if you always smell of chilli mate," Chris said.

"Hey, I do okay. I've got a date tonight. Do you?" Andy said before biting into this sandwich.

"Internet girls don't count."

Andy swallowed. "What do you mean they don't count? Don't knock it until you've tried it, pal. This one's really cute."

Chris chuckled. "She's probably a guy dressed in drag."

"Hey, that was once! These days I only meet for a quick wine or coffee, just in case. Rule number one of internet dating … have an escape plan."

"Oh by the way, they arrested that woman you dated last month," Chris said.

"This is one of your stupid jokes right?"

"No it's true. They picked her up for possession. When they strip-searched her at the station and lifted the back of her skirt, they found sixty kilo's of crack."

"Plonker!" Andy took another bite of his sandwich savouring the chilli and ignoring Chris's laughter.

Andy's passion for chilli had led him, at one time or another, to most of the shops that sold them in the Wellington region. Andy's current favourite, *Locos Jalapeños*, came in a distinctively shaped jar that was slightly wider at the top than at the bottom and had a bright yellow screw-cap with the picture of a fat green chilli on it. Normally, he purchased them three or four jars at a time from a shop near the northern end of Hopper Street, on the outskirts of the CBD.

The kidnapper had used *Locos Jalapeños* jars to send the severed fingers of eight-year-old Leonard Bourne to his parents. When Andy saw the police photos, he'd identified them immediately.

The use of four identical jars had been one of the few clues police had in the case. Officers contacted the Auckland firm that imported the chillies from Mexico, but the importer's database contained over 580 shops, wholesalers, supermarkets, and delicatessens in New Zealand, thirty-two in downtown Wellington alone that stocked them.

The lead detective on the Bourne case, Detective Inspector Robert Warner, didn't have the manpower available to put a surveillance team on every outlet. Nor was there any evidence to support Andy's theory that chillies were addictive and the culprit would return to buy more. For all Warner knew, the jars could have come from anywhere. The two ransom notes produced no leads either. They were just a few words cut from the local paper stuck onto plain paper with a brand of PVA glue that could be bought in any supermarket, hardware shop or discounter. There were no fingerprints. No DNA. Nothing.

Although Chris and Andy weren't one of the teams officially assigned to the Bourne case, whenever they had a bit of spare time they'd stake out the shop on Hopper Street. Andy's bizarre hunches had paid off before so, despite long odds the kidnapper would show up, they watched. After tailing a couple of dodgy looking *Locos Jalapeños* buyers, and investigating them discretely without result, Chris was beginning to think they were wasting their time. Then one afternoon, their watching, against all odds and realistic expectation, paid off.

After following a suspicious looking guy to an apartment building in Tinakori Road, the detectives went to the balcony of the next door neighbour. The curtains of the suspect's apartment were drawn, but a window was open a crack.

As Chris and Andy listened at the window, Andy thought he could hear a child crying. When a man yelled 'shut the fuck up' they both heard it. The two detectives knew a child crying, closed curtains, and an angry man, wasn't conclusive evidence, but the tone of the man's voice, and their instincts, gave them enough reason to make an urgent call to Detective Inspector Warner.

Warner, praying that the two detective's hunch was correct, called a judge and pleaded with him to issue a search warrant. Luckily, the judge was in a good mood that day and within an hour, D.I. Warner, his assistant Detective Deborah Green, and members of the Armed Offenders Squad raided the apartment.

The rest is history. Warner played hero on the six o'clock news, describing to an enthralled nation how determined police work had enabled the suspect's arrest and rescued a child from the hands of a monster. At the same time, Chris and Andy, accompanied by a few other detectives, celebrated the arrest with a few beers down at the local pub when their shift finished. Neither man needed to buy a round that night.

The kidnapper, Gerard Williamson, appeared in court the following day charged with numerous offences. The Judge remanded him into custody, and ordered him to undergo a psychiatric examination prior to a preliminary hearing.

Leonard Bourne, missing four fingers, traumatized, and in need of counselling, spent the night in hospital, his parents by his side. His mum and dad, although relieved their son was safe would take weeks if not months to recover from the ordeal.

The only positives to come out of the whole affair were firstly, Leonard wouldn't be forced to take piano lessons, and secondly, Chris and Andy got some much needed brownie points back at the station.

The two detectives had been working day shift when the Bourne case broke, stuck in a stuffy car or office much of the time. Moving around town tested their patience, and rush hour seemed to last forever. Cars and buses congested the streets, while shoppers, tourists, and sandwich boards, clogged the footpaths.

Luckily for them, being primarily involved in drug enforcement allowed them a certain amount of flexibility. In summer, when their workload allowed, they preferred to work nights. Daylight savings gave them plenty of time in the early evenings to enjoy the sun or their favourite sports.

Kayaking on the harbour, jogging, riding the numerous mountain bike trails, sailing, windsurfing or any number of leisure activities the Wellington area provided were popular.

Night shifts often started with a glorious sunset and the smell of spices emanating from Wellington's many restaurants. They then progressed to bright lights, nightclubs, cool sea breezes, and an almost tolerable traffic level.

Chris and Andy enjoyed the cat-like existence of hunting at night, secretly watching, waiting, and then pouncing on their prey. When working nights they could hide in the shadows, and be seen only when they wanted to be seen. Night gave them the illusion of anonymity, of safety, and invulnerability.

At night, no excuse on earth could explain why some sleaze was somewhere he shouldn't be, especially with his trousers around his knees, and a fifteen-year-old runaway sucking his cock in return for drugs or alcohol. No reasonable doubt, convicted as charged.

**********

Gerard Williamson had been in custody since his arrest for kidnapping the previous Wednesday. As he sat on the bed in his cell, he looked at the concrete floor and grubby grey walls that had been white in a previous life. The front of the cell had iron bars and a door with a narrow slot in its centre. At approximately two and a half metres wide, and four meters long, the cell had a thin mattress on a metal frame bolted to the wall. A stainless steel toilet, with no seat or lid, stood against the back wall, and a small hand basin with a single tap completed the cubicle's meagre appointments. Gerard's cell was one of many in a long row that made up the prison's remand wing.

The old, damp prison sat on a hill overlooking the city. Only the Corrections Department could build a building in such prime position, without a single window taking advantage of the view. Luckily for Gerard, it was summer. He'd heard stories about the cold drafty winters up at Mount Crawford, but hoped he wouldn't be here long enough to find out if the rumours were true.

Sound emanated from every cell, creating a constant din. The shouts and groans of the other prisoners were a constant irritation. Gerard hated it. After a five-day methamphetamine binge, Gerard found sleep hard to come by despite his tiredness.

Thirty-five years old, and of medium height and weight, Gerard had dark hair and brown eyes that overlooked a thin nose.

Gerard's hand shook as he lit another cigarette from the butt of the one he'd just finished. Then he picked at the scab forming on his scalp where he'd taken a knock during his arrest. Gerard felt like shit on a stick, even after the shower and shave authorities had allowed him earlier that morning. The dark drooping bags under his eyes made him look far older than his years.

Facing up to seventeen years for kidnapping, aggravated assault, attempted murder, and a multitude of drug and other charges, Gerard cursed himself for screwing up and landing himself in this stinking hole. He rocked back and forth, the cigarette clamped between two yellow fingers, sniffing his runny nose.

*Attempted murder, like fuck! If I'd wanted to kill the kid he'd be dead. I wish I had topped the noisy little shit. At least then I wouldn't be sitting in this stinking hole.*

Gerard jump up and marched to the door of his cell. "Where's my fucking lawyer!"

The guard should have escorted Gerard to the interview room over an hour ago. As he waited, Gerard chain-smoked and rocked back and forth. His nerves had had it, and all this waiting didn't help.

"Fuck, fuck, fuck."

Nathan Williamson, Gerard's father, had hired the lawyer. After his arrest, Gerard had pleaded with his father to find him representation. Nathan had reluctantly engaged Rod Jackson from a law firm that had offices in the same building a few floors above his own.

Gerard wasn't very impressed with his father's choice thus far. Jackson just seemed to be going through the motions. He didn't listen. He was arrogant and always seemed in a hurry to leave, even when Gerard still had unanswered questions. Gerard had hoped for better. Supposedly his father knew about lawyers. After all, he'd been one himself until a career change had been forced upon him.

These days Nathan Williamson called himself a 'finance and mortgage broker'. But in reality, 'scumbag' fit his job description more aptly. With the gift of the gab learned through years of court appearances, he now charmed retired couples into refinancing their family homes through a number of less than reputable private companies he represented.

These finance companies had a scheme where retirees could keep their family home, gradually reducing their equity in it over time, thus giving them the extra cash when they needed it to buy a few luxuries, pay for a hip replacement, or take the odd holiday to the Australian Gold Coast.

Encouraged by the finance company, and often much quicker than they'd thought possible, the retirees would eat up their equity, and the property would end up on the market. The higher than normal interest rates, and exorbitant administration fees, combined with the finance company's predisposition to force a sale as soon as the client's equity reached an arbitrary minimum safe threshold, created an opportunity for Williamson and his less than honourable associates to cash in.

Wanting to avoid the embarrassment of a mortgagee sale, and in some cases not knowing the value of their property, the retirees would be persuaded to sell prior to auction. This enabled Williamson and his cronies, through a series of third party companies, to swoop in with a cash offer and purchase the property below the market price. After a quick and shoddy makeover, they would on sell for a substantial profit. The way property prices continued to rise, they couldn't fail to make money.

Gerard was a chip off his old man's block, having inherited his father's desire for easy money and his lack of a conscience.

While he was working as a lawyer in the late nineties, Nathan Williamson had embezzled hundreds of thousands of dollars from one of his employer's trust accounts.

After sneakily obtaining the passwords of both the trust accountant, and the firm's office manager, Nathan Williamson shifted varying amounts of money through a complex series of electronic transfers and shell companies into a number of offshore accounts. When things went pear shaped, Nathan Williamson simply denied any involvement.

Nathan knew the firm would never be able prove anything beyond a reasonable doubt, even if they suspected his involvement. Nathan also knew the shell companies and numbered accounts he'd set up were untraceable. Discovery of the embezzlement was inevitable, so Nathan had taken particular care to cover his tracks.

The law firm, wanting to maintain its reputation, went to great lengths to keep the embarrassing episode from both their clients, and the public. Although the firm's auditors had no concrete proof, they had concluded after an extensive in-house investigation, that Williamson was the most likely culprit.

The partners decided that taking the hit and covering the losses themselves would be a cheaper solution in the long run. The bad publicity a trial would bring, along with the resulting loss of clientele, was not a scenario the firm wanted to explore. Their hard-earned reputation was worth far more than a quarter of a million dollars.

The company did make certain however, that Williamson, the office manager, and the trust accountant, would never work for another law firm in New Zealand.

While Nathan Williamson went on vacation to the Cayman Islands and started planning his next career move, the two duped employees went to work for whatever fast-food franchise would hire them.

********

Andy heard another unit pick up the call. "Phew, thanks boys. Hey Chris, what say we go for that coffee now?"

"Sounds like a plan," Chris said jumping into the car. "I could do with a caffeine fix and something to eat."

Chris hadn't been sleeping well since the Bourne case, and he'd never been one to eat first thing in the morning. A cup of coffee and a toothbrush was all he managed for breakfast most mornings.

Chris yawned as he drove them to Expressaholic on Cuba Street, one place they were assured of getting a decent brew.

"Hey, did you know that Wellington has more restaurants and cafés per capita than New York?" Andy said with a hint of pride in his voice.

"Yeah? Not surprising I suppose. They seem to be springing up all over the place."

"Have you tried that new Cambodian place up Dixon Street yet?"

"Nah, I don't do spicy food." Chris replied. "Give me a big fat juicy steak any day."

Andy screwed up his nose. "Do you have any idea how long it takes to digest a steak?"

"Hey, mate, I eat veggies too. It's just that chillies isn't one of them."

**********

The guard escorted Gerard down from his cell, through a

small reception lobby, and locked him into one of the six interview rooms to wait yet again. The room, bare apart from a table bolted to the floor and two plastic chairs, smelled of damp. Pockmarked linoleum graced the floor, and the walls were the same grubby grey as the cells in the remand wing.

The lobby guard finally unlocked the door and let in Rod Jackson just before 11:00 a.m. Jackson wore a dark blue suit, carried an expensive leather briefcase, and wore a stylish hat to keep off the summer sun.

The two men's eyes were level when Gerard stood up and held out his hand. Jackson ignored the proffered handshake and walked around him to the table, taking the seat facing the door. Jackson offered no apology for his lateness.

Taking a file from his briefcase, Jackson got straight down to it.

"Although your father's prepared to pay for your defence he's instructed me to inform you he doesn't want any further contact from you after the trial."

"The old bastard's cutting me off?"

"An interesting turn of phrase considering the circumstances … but yes."

Gerard hated Jackson's attitude, hated his smarmy smile, hated how he strutted when he walked, and especially hated the way he seemed to enjoy passing on his father's message.

Gerard glared at the lawyer. "My father's a hypocritical prick! He's been in plenty of trouble himself you know. His whole business revolves around fucking people over … hurting them."

"Look I'm just paid to do my job. Your relationship with your father is none of my concern."

Gerard could just imagine his father trying to screw him over.

*The old bastard's probably got Jackson in his back pocket, instructed him to do the absolute minimum. Fuck, for all I know the gutless tosser could be trying to get me convicted.*

While Gerard imagined the worst, Jackson took another file out of his briefcase and put it on the table. It was Gerard's psychiatric report.

"It's not looking good," the lawyer explained. "The

psychiatrist has deemed you fit to stand trial. He says that although you're seriously disturbed, you know the difference between right and wrong, and therefore have to defend the charges in court."

Gerard knew he wasn't crazy, but this wasn't the news he wanted to hear.

*I'm going to get shafted big time if I don't get out of here. But how?*

Gerard looked at the lawyer, his mind working furiously. Then an inkling of a plan began to take shape.

*Jackson and I are roughly the same size and shape ...*

"You do realise the chance of escaping imprisonment is virtually nonexistent. That's why you should consider making a deal. You might get a reduced sentence in exchange for a guilty plea. It's the sensible option."

"What and do eight or ten years?"

"If this case goes to trial, you could get seventeen years, or even worse, preventative detention. With that they can keep you locked up indefinitely. Is that what you want?"

"No of course not but ...

"There are no buts. You need to start showing some remorse for what you've done otherwise any deals will be off the table. You'll also have to agree to undergo extensive therapy while in prison. Come here let me show you what I plan to propose to the prosecutors."

*Ten fucking years? More therapy?*

Gerard got up from his chair and walked to the small window in the interview room's door. There was no sign of the second guard. Most likely, he'd be on a break or off escorting another prisoner. The remaining guard was busy reading something lying on the counter in front of him.

Gerard wondered how much time he'd have to execute the sketchy plan he had roughed out in his head.

*Not long. I'll just have to wing it*

Gerard had heard too many horror stories about the prison system, and doubted he'd survive it. Even when put into protective custody the other inmates could find ways of getting to you, hurting you. Even the most hardened criminals loved their kids. Many would go to extraordinary lengths to punish inmates they suspected of crimes against children.

Turning from the window, Gerard looked back towards the table where Jackson had spread out some papers for him to review. Gerard walked over and went behind the lawyer, acting as though he was going to read the report over the lawyer's shoulder. Instead, Gerard clasped both hands together into a double fist.

*Nothing to lose, so here goes.*

Swinging his arms like an axe, Gerard brought his clenched fists down as hard as he could on the back of the lawyer's neck. The blow sent the lawyer crashing off his chair to the floor. As the dazed Jackson got to his hands and knees, Gerard rocked back on one leg like a goal kicker, and then swung his foot forward with as much force as he could muster, kicking the lawyer squarely in the face.

*Take that you prick!*

Gerard, afraid the lobby guard might have heard the thwack of Gerard's foot imploding Jackson's cheek or the lawyer crashing to the floor, ran to the window and peered out. There was still no sign of the second guard, and the first guard remained seated behind the counter engrossed in his reading.

Moving swiftly, Gerard grabbed some tissues out of his pocket and wiped the blood off the lawyer's face. Then Gerard stuffed some tissue paper into each of Jackson's nostrils to stem the blood flow, and protect the suit. Jackson didn't move a muscle.

Straightening the lawyer's legs, Gerard took off Jackson's shoes, unbuckled his belt, and pulled off his trousers. Rolling Jackson onto his stomach, Gerard pulled off the lawyer's jacket. Puffing from exertion, Gerard rolled Jackson over again, and undid his tie. Then he quickly unbuttoned Jackson's crisp white shirt. After doing the flip-flop with the lawyer a few more times, Gerard had removed all but his singlet and boxers. Then Gerard undressed. Taking his shoes and prison overalls off, Gerard quickly dragged the overalls up over Jackson's legs, and worked the lawyer's arms into the sleeves. Then he put his prison-issue shoes onto the lawyer's feet.

The lawyer's clothes fit Gerard perfectly. After dressing in the suit, and putting on the lawyer's shoes and tie, Gerard picked up the fallen chair and placed its back facing the door. He then grabbed Jackson under the armpits and hoisted him up onto the chair. Arranging the unconscious lawyer in as natural a pose as his inert body would allow, Gerard draped one of the lawyer's legs over the other, and placed Jackson's elbow on the edge of the table. To complete the illusion, Gerard wedged a lit cigarette, between Jackson's fingers.

As Gerard stood near the door, he looked at the scene critically, trying to see it from the guard's perspective. It wasn't perfect, but it would have to do.

Gerard put on the lawyer's hat, and stuffed the papers from the table into the briefcase before giving his face a quick wipe with the back of his sleeve. Then Gerard picked up the briefcase from the table and walked near the door. He had one last look at the scene, saw the smoke curling up from Jackson's motionless fingers, and rang the buzzer for the guard to let him out of the interview room.

"Don't forget to breathe," Gerard whispered to himself.

Standing side-on to the door, Gerard pulled the brim of the hat down as far as he could without it being obvious. When he heard the guard's footsteps, he turned his head at a slight angle, hiding most of his face.

As the door opened, the guard looked across the room. "Hurry up and finish that smoke Williamson. George will be here in a minute to escort you back to your cell."

Gerard turned towards the door, swung the briefcase forward, and strutted with as much confidence as he could muster into the lobby, slapping the visitor's I.D. tag onto the counter as he passed. As Gerard continued toward the exit with his back to the guard, he waved a cursory goodbye over his shoulder, along with a mumbled 'thank you' and stood by the exit, tapping his foot and doing his best to look like a man in a hurry to get back to the office.

The guard, impatient to get back to his race book, went behind the counter and buzzed the door open and a very relieved Gerard Williamson walked out into the sunshine a free man.

As Gerard hurried down the path towards the car park a hundred metres away, he couldn't believe his luck. Still, he wasn't in the clear yet. Before the guards discovered his deception, Gerard had to get down the hill and into town. The police would have time to set up roadblocks if he didn't move quickly. Only once he'd disappeared into the city's southern suburbs would Gerard be in the clear.

Picking up the pace, Gerard walked like an important man, with important things to do, and important places to be. Not a difficult part to play really, for in Gerard's mind, that's exactly what he was.

Gerard looked for a familiar vehicle. One he knew he could hotwire. He felt the weight of the briefcase in his hand. It would be a perfect tool for breaking a car window if need be. Then ten or so cars down the first row, Gerard noticed a Toyota Corolla with its back window partially open.

Gerard squeezed his hand through the back window, around the pillar to the front door, and popped the lock. He dropped the briefcase on the passenger seat, ripped the wiring out from underneath the dash, grabbed the ignition wires and started the car. Then, as calmly as possible, he put the car into gear and drove out of the parking lot and down the hill. Five minutes later, he joined the airport traffic streaming towards the city.

**********

The guard, having let Williamson's lawyer out, made a quick call to the T.A.B. He had just enough time to put a twenty-dollar bet on *Hoof Hearted* to win in the second race at Ellerslie. Already forty dollars down after the first two races, the guard needed a change of luck. If he didn't have a win soon, he'd be explaining to his wife how he'd lost the money earmarked for his daughter's birthday present, and most likely looking for a new place to live. She'd already threatened to kick him out if he gambled again.

A few minutes later, there was a jingle of keys in the door on the far side of the lobby. Turning down the radio, the guard put the race book out of sight under the counter and nodded to George as he came through the door.

"Williamson in three is ready to go back up. His lawyer left ten minutes ago."

George pulled his keys from the retractable clip on his belt, walked over to interview room three, slotted a key into the lock, and opened the door.

"What the hell?" George said taking in the scene.

As he walked around the table, George saw Rod Jackson's burnt fingers, smashed teeth, and broken nose. "This isn't Williamson!" He yelled through the door. "Hit the alarm you fuckwit, you've let out the wrong guy!"

"Ah Jesus!" The guard reached under the counter and hit the alarm button. He now had two problems. *Hoof Hearted* had just lost by a nose.

# CHAPTER 3 - MONDAY AFTERNOON

Gerard turned out of the main traffic flow and into the suburb of Kilbirnie just after midday. Although close to town, he thought it best not to drive a stolen car into the city. Turning down a quiet street, he pulled the car to the curb under the shade of an overhanging pohutukawa tree, but left the engine idling. After a quick glance up and down the street, he twisted slightly in his seat and flipped the catches on the briefcase.

Under the papers Gerard had thrown haphazardly into the briefcase, he found a wallet, some manila folders, and a set of keys. The wallet contained close to two hundred dollars in notes, two credit cards, and the normal assortment of odds and sods. After transferring the wallet to his trouser pocket, Gerard took the papers that related to his case and folded them a couple of time before slotting them neatly into the inside pocket of the jacket.

Gerard knew he had to dump the car soon, but he wanted to find a spot where an abandoned car wouldn't attract attention. He didn't want to give the police any extra help in tracking him. If it took the police a few days to find the car, they might think he'd driven it out of the Wellington area altogether.

Gerard closed the briefcase and put the car into gear. After driving around for a few minutes, he pulled into the visitor's car park of a modest two-story apartment block on Onepu Road.

It was a good spot. The car wasn't visible from the street, and it could take days before one of the residents realised the car had been abandoned. Tossing the lawyer's hat and briefcase into the back seat, Gerard got out, closed the door, and started walking. It was only a short distance to the Kilbirnie shops. There he'd catch a bus into the city.

Gerard figured he wouldn't have long to wait. The main bus depot was nearby, and buses ran regularly into town from here. Tucking himself into the corner of the bus shelter, out of view from passersby, he puffed on a cigarette and waited.

As he waited, Gerard praised himself for having the foresight to rent a bolt hole some months back. His natural caution had told him a safe-house might come in handy one day. Ever since his parents had forced him into therapy as a child, he'd done his best to stay one move ahead in the game. Now, because of this forward planning, he had a place to hide and think about his next move, a private place, unknown to family or the police.

The bus arrived just as Gerard stubbed out his second cigarette. Nearly empty, except for a couple of older women carrying shopping bags, a young man lugging a school satchel, and four or five others, Gerard paid the fare and settled in amongst them for the twenty-minute journey into town.

As they neared The Basin Reserve, Gerard started to sweat. He took off the jacket and thought briefly about dumping it, but the pockets came in handy, and it fit so well, he couldn't bring himself to leave such a quality garment behind.

Holding the jacket in his lap, Gerard looked out the window and remembered the good times he'd spent at the Basin watching the cricket.

The Basin Reserve had once been a lagoon. The city council at the time had been considering digging a kilometre long canal linking it to Wellington Harbour when an earthquake in 1855 spoiled their plans. The quake uplifted the land, and turned the basin into swampland. So, instead of digging a canal, the Council decided to fill in the swamp and turn the Basin Reserve into the sports ground it is today.

Gerard had enjoyed many summer afternoons as a teenager, sitting on the grassy bank during matches. There were always plenty of kids hanging around, which made it a fertile venue for Gerard's vivid imagination. He spent many happy hours daydreaming about what he could do to them, given the opportunity.

The number of spectators made it impossible for him to attempt anything at the Basin Reserve itself, but once, after a match, he dragged a young boy who'd been walking home alone into the bushes, terrorising him for ten minutes or so, and breaking one of his fingers in the process.

Having control over others excited Gerard. It made him feel

good to inflict pain, very good indeed.

When the bus arrived at Courtenay Place a few minutes later, Gerard, along with six or seven others, hopped off. He wanted to lose himself in the crowd so, throwing the jacket over his shoulder, Gerard walked off trying his best to blend in.

As he walked, Gerard kept an eye out for cops. He couldn't risk taking a cab, the driver might recognise him once news of his escape hit the papers, but it didn't matter. On a fine day like today, with all the other activity about, Gerard doubted anyone would take an interest in him.

The cops wouldn't know which direction he'd gone so Gerard figured any coordinated search would take a while to mobilise. Having missed lunch, he thought he might stop at one of the cafés on Oriental Parade and pick up something to eat along the way.

*Spicy nachos with jalapeño will hit the spot.*

Turning left at Downstage Theatre, Gerard walked down Cambridge Terrace and past the supermarket toward Oriental Parade for a couple of minutes, and then turned right along Oriental Parade itself to join the throng milling about on the waterfront. Amongst the crowd he saw a few kids, but he didn't have time to linger and fantasise. Right now getting something inside his stomach and then getting off the street were his main priorities.

As Gerard walked he watched the crowd, scanning the street ahead for danger. Some of the pedestrians had stopped along the sea wall and were looking at the yachts moored in the Port Nicholson Marina. A busker, strumming a guitar and singing, worked the crowd, his hat lying on the footpath ready for donations.

Happy families made Gerard want to puke. His childhood had been a nightmare of parents screaming at each other, his father smacking him, calling him a little monster, and bi-weekly therapy sessions.

Passing the Freyberg Pool, Gerard looked left towards the harbour. The sun made the harbour sparkle with a thousand pinpoints of light, and every very last one of them made Gerard's eyes hurt. He looked down and patted his pockets hoping the lawyer had left a pair of sunglasses in one of them, but there were none to be found.

"Fuck, fuck, fuck," Gerard mumbled under his breath.

As he looked up again, a police car appeared from behind the coffee caravan by the main beach. His heart nearly jumped out of his chest. Pretending to take interest in the Cook Strait ferry moving towards its berth on the far side of the harbour Gerard turned his face away and prayed the two officers in the car hadn't seen him.

Once the car had passed, Gerard twisted around to watch them, expecting the brake lights to go on at any moment. Holding his breath he watched until the car continued around the corner and out of sight.

To be on the safe side, Gerard scampered across the street and entered a café. He sat at a table near the back facing the door where he could see the street.

While he waited for a staff member his stomach rumbled. When the young man arrived to take his order, Gerard ordered Nachos with a side dish of chilli peppers.

"Jalapeños if you've got them."

The meal didn't take long to arrive. Forking the extra chillies over the sour cream topping, Gerard started to eat, relishing the spicy heat.

After the meal, Gerard had a quick coffee, paid the bill with some of the lawyer's cash, and continued on his way.

In the distance Gerard could see a narrow roadway climbing up the cliff face. This would be the more direct route to his apartment, but if police spotted him going up that route he'd have nowhere to run. Instead, Gerard opted to use Grass Street, most of which comprised a pedestrian walkway running up the hill through the trees. A better option by far, he'd be less visible to police, and out of the heat of the sun.

After a fifteen-minute uphill slog, Gerard reached the concrete building that contained his and eleven other small apartments. The building had three floors with four apartments per floor. Being on the back of the top floor meant Gerard's apartment didn't get much afternoon sun or views of the city like those at the front, but that didn't concern Gerard. His priority was a quiet place where the landlord didn't snoop around.

Gerard shunned the lift and started up the stairs. At the top of the stairs, he did a U-turn, walked past his door on the right, and reached a small alcove that held three terracotta pots overflowing with succulents. Gerard dug his fingers deep into the potting mix of one pot and came up with a key covered in clear kitchen wrap. Returning to the door to his apartment, he removed the plastic, and slotted the key into the lock. The key turned. The tumblers clicked, and the door opened.

**********

Andy sat at his desk reviewing some current case files, when his cell phone rang.

"Thompson."

He listened carefully for a moment then shook his head in disbelief. "You must be joking!" He listened a few moments more and then closed his phone and shut his eyes. "Fucking hell," he mumbled.

When Chris came into the office moments later carrying two cups of coffee, Andy looked up. "Hey, you won't believe this. Gerard Williamson's done a runner from the remand wing. Kicked the shit out of his lawyer, stole his clothes, and walked right out the fucking door!"

"How the hell did that happen?"

"One of the guards didn't check properly."

"You mean the soon to be unemployed guard that's just done a swan dive into a very deep pool of shit?"

"Yep that's the one. The APB will be out in a few minutes."

"Just what we need, another loon on the loose."

The politically correct term for Gerard Williamson's condition was 'Sadistic Personality Disorder', but 'loon' worked just fine for Andy. SPD was a condition that often manifested itself in the young, usually beginning with the mistreatment of animals. People with this disorder derive intense pleasure from causing pain and suffering to others. In extreme cases like Gerard's, they progress from hurting animals as children, to hurting people as they mature.

The thought of Gerard running around the community again gave Andy the shits. Andy had read articles about SPD. One mentioned Prince Vlad the Impaler, the inspiration for the original Count Dracula stories, and a classic case of SPD. Prince Vlad, a sadistic bastard of the highest order, enjoyed impaling the local citizens on long wooden stakes at the top of a nearby hill. The prince would then sit and eat lunch surrounded by their screams of agony.

It could take hours for some to die. The article mentioned that during one such meal, an underling was overheard by the Prince saying that 'impaling people wasn't a very nice thing to do' (or words to that affect). It didn't take long for the underling to discover his mistake, finding himself impaled on a stake of his very own shortly thereafter. The Prince, it seemed, wasn't a fan of unsolicited comments that were critical of his favourite pastime.

Andy shuddered when he thought about it, but was startled out of his daydream by Chris.

"Hey, seeing we've got the jump on the others, what say we join the hunt? We might just spot the prick. Especially if he's on foot heading towards town. An hour looking, then we'll get back to work. Okay?"

"Sure, no worries," Andy said, still thinking about Prince Vlad. "Let's cruise around the bays towards the airport. You never know your luck in the big city."

"If I was Williamson, I'd try to steal a car, wouldn't you?"

"That would make sense. He got done once for car conversion as a teenager didn't he?"

Chris nodded. "I'd better drive then. If we spot him going the other way we'll never catch him if you're behind the wheel."

As the two detectives passed Te Papa, The National Museum, on their way towards Oriental Parade the APB came over the radio confirming Williamson's escape. Their slight advantage in the race to find Williamson had just evaporated.

**********

Blondie stood as tall as many of the male officers she worked with. She had shoulder length dark hair and a shapely figure. She'd gained her nickname early in her career when, on a whim, she decided to put a blond streak in her hair. The streak, coupled with her given name being Deborah, like the famous singer of the same name, was all the boys at the station needed. Even though the streak had long gone, for some reason the nickname had stuck. Not that Blondie was 'blond' in the bimbo sense. Those who made that assumption did so at their peril. Her sharp tongue and sarcastic wit had made fools of those who'd patronised or doubted her ability on numerous occasions.

A few of the braver men around the station had asked her out, but since transferring to Wellington, she'd resisted all temptations. A romantic entanglement with a colleague had caused her problems in the past. Blondie didn't plan on making the same mistake again.

Pleased to have such a capable assistant, D.I. Warner and Blondie had fallen into a friendship of sorts, not that Blondie pushed it. Warner out ranked her by two grades which made true friendship difficult. But that didn't stop them showing a high level of mutual respect and camaraderie. Blondie put her all into the job, determined to make an impact in the decidedly male dominated culture of the New Zealand Police. Her work ethic and positive attitude impressed Warner.

Warner and Blondie were fighting a stack of paperwork in Warner's office when the phone rang. Shortly after Warner answered the call, his face turned the colour of Pinot Noir and he slammed the phone down.

"Shit!"

Blondie could see a vein throbbing below the skin of his forehead as Warner put his face in his hands and growled like a dog, shaking his head back and forth in frustration.

Blondie had never seen Warner so upset. "Don't blow a valve boss. Surely it can't be that bad."

Warner looked up, distress obvious in his eyes. "Gerard

Williamson has escaped. He knocked out his lawyer and swapped clothes. Some idiot guard didn't notice the difference and let the bastard out."

"Oh dear," Blondie said. "I bet the warden is dusting off his guillotine as we speak."

"Heads rolling won't help catch Williamson. We were lucky the first time. Now we're back to square one."

As the Detective Inspector in charge of the Bourne case, Warner knew he'd be asked to run the hunt for Gerard Williamson again. It wasn't a proposition he looked forward to.

Warner thumped his desk. "Come to think of it Blondie, the guillotine sounds a bloody good idea. Hell, give me the opportunity and I'll pull the bloody lever myself."

The guard's stupid mistake meant another round of frantic days and sleepless nights for Warner and his team. It wouldn't be easy finding someone like Gerard whose intelligence and years of practiced secrecy made him different to the average criminal. Add Gerard's tendency towards violence into the mix, and it makes for a scary situation.

Gerard, and what he might do, certainly scared Warner. What lunacy would he get into his head this time? Would he abduct another child? Would he stay in the area or would he flee? Anything was possible.

Having been in the house with Leonard Bourne's parents when the third finger arrived, Warner had seen the look on their faces, had heard the wails of grief from the boy's mother, and had watched tears of helplessness run down the father's cheeks.

*Only an animal could do that to a child.*

Warner put a hand on his stomach, and winced slightly. He pulled out the top drawer of his desk and rummaged around for some antacid tablets. Remembering the sight of Leonard Bourne's bloody little finger in the jar, and how close they'd come to losing the boy made his guts churn.

Frustration had become a constant companion during those days of fruitless searching. Most nights Warner found himself up late in his book-lined study, sitting behind an old rimu desk reading files, a bottle of scotch at his elbow, hoping the drink would dull his senses sufficiently so that he could go upstairs to bed with at least a chance of getting some sleep.

As Warner stared blankly at the opposite wall thinking, Blondie grabbed the keyboard and spun Warner's monitor around. "I'll update the main server and flag Williamson's file urgent. Maybe we'll get lucky and a unit will pick him up before he gets too far."

"I doubt luck will have much to do with it." Warner replied. "Gerard will be twice as cautious now ... and that makes him twice as dangerous."

Both Warner and Blondie had read Gerard's psyche report after his arrest. Gerard Williamson had an estimated I.Q. of 145, which put him in the top 3% of the population. But being bright didn't mean he was normal. Like train tracks, madness and genius often run side by side. The problem is, every now and then there's a fault in the system. In Gerard's case, his mind had derailed shortly after leaving the station.

Gerard liked hurting people, and did so with gusto. As other clever people solved impossible equations or discovered planets around some distant binary star, Gerard dreamed of secateurs, blood, and pain.

Police knew Gerard had been in treatment for a number of years as a youngster. Nathan had told police all about his son's problems when he was first interviewed after Gerard's arrest.

"Amazing how little parents know about their children sometimes." Blondie said. "Gerard's out killing the neighbourhood pets, and his parents think everything's hunky-dory."

Warner nodded in agreement. "What scares me is the ease in which Gerard snatched the boy from his school. Makes me want to keep my son at home."

"I don't blame you," Blondie said.

Although she didn't have children, it didn't take much imagination to understand how Warner felt. The teachers at Leonard Bourne's school had known nothing of the abduction until it was too late.

To get away so cleanly, police assumed Leonard Bourne's

kidnapper had watched the school and gotten to know their routine. Leonard was just the unlucky kid who went to get the football. The number plates of the van used in the abduction were covered in mud. The teachers could only watch as the rear of a white van, disappeared into the distance.

As Warner and Blondie sat discussing their next move, a uniformed officer entered the office and dropped a pile of papers on his desk. "Missing Corolla from the prison car park, they reckon it must have been Williamson."

"Oh great. Any idea how long it's been gone?" Warner asked.

"At least an hour ... could be longer. The details have been sent out to the patrols."

"He could be anywhere by now," Blondie said.

Warner did not look happy. "Now we'll have to dig up something we missed the first time around, or hope like hell Gerard makes a mistake."

**********

Nathan Williamson heard of his son's escape on National Radio's three o'clock news. The breaking story led the program, going into considerable detail about the vicious assault on Gerard's lawyer as well as dragging up the sordid details of the Bourne case all over again. Considering the public interest that had surrounded Leonard Bourne's kidnapping, and the police search for him, it wasn't surprising. Bourne's kidnapping and mutilation had been one of the year's biggest stories. Like so many other countries, New Zealand had become a nation of ghouls.

Nathan sighed and put his head in his hands when he heard the news. Sickened by the things his son had done, Nathan hoped Gerard's would be convicted and sentenced to a lengthy term in prison. Prison was where Gerard belonged. His son was damaged goods and beyond repair.

Nathan couldn't believe the ineptitude of the prison service. Pulling a tissue from his pocket, he wiped the sweat from his forehead. Like the last time Gerard played up, Nathan had no doubt he'd be hearing from the cops again soon.

Although Gerard's arrest for the kidnapping and brutal disfigurement of Leonard Bourne had been a shock to Nathan, he'd always known, deep down, something like this was a possibility. When Gerard was ten, the discovery of a mutilated cat, partly buried in the back yard of their Auckland home, first alerted the Williamsons to their son's problem. It wasn't however, until they investigated the burial site more closely, that Gerard's parents understood the full extent of their son's illness. The site they'd originally thought contained a single shallow grave was in fact a deep hole, and the cat on top, just the tip of a very large and hideous iceberg.

Approximately twenty animals from their neighbourhood had mysteriously disappeared over the previous year. Gerard's parents didn't need to dig far before realising this grave contained most, if not all of them.

At the age of five or six, Gerard had pulled the wings and legs off insects he'd caught, giggling all the while. With the discovery of the buried animals, it all finally clicked. They'd raised a monster.

The Williamsons decided to move house. Then they'd get their son some much-needed help. After some discussion, Gerard's parents decided to leave their grieving neighbours in the dark, opting instead to plant a memorial kowhai tree on the mass grave to hide their son's atrocities. At least with all the Fido and Fluffy fertilizer the tree had for nourishment, the Williamsons knew it would grow well.

After selling up in Auckland, the Williamsons moved to Paremata, a small beach suburb up the coast from Wellington. They purchased an old rambling villa that had a small section opposite the beach. Native bush abounded on the hills, and the beach was gently sloping and safe for swimming.

Once settled in their new home, Gerard's parents engaged a child psychologist for the boy. After three years of therapy, everyone thought Gerard's treatment had been successful. No pets had gone missing in the neighbourhood. Gerard had even made a few friends at school and had started to act like other thirteen year olds. Unfortunately, and unbeknownst to his parents and therapist, acting was exactly what Gerard had been doing.

The Williamsons, convinced Gerard's therapy had done the trick, got on with their lives. But Gerard had fooled them all. He'd learned to disguise his true feelings. Rather than curing Gerard, it had taught him how others expected him to act, and how best to hide his wants and desires. The whole experience made Gerard realise he had to go further from home if he wanted to experiment on animals, and that he had to hide his handiwork better. Going over old ground with the psychiatrist also made Gerard realise how much pleasure he got from remembering his earlier behaviour. Sometimes he could barely keep himself from moaning in pleasure as he recounted some blood-soaked episode, re-running it in his mind as if it were yesterday. The three years of therapy had been very instructional indeed for Gerard, just not in the way his parents intended.

At 3:30 p.m. Nathan got a call from his secretary informing him that Peter Slater, a senior partner from the law firm he'd engaged to defend his son, wanted to see him. Nathan knew Slater would be outraged at his son's brutal assault on one of his staff.

"Tell him I'm across town in a meeting Sheryl," Nathan said. "I can't deal with him at the moment."

After a few moments delay, Sheryl rang him back. "Slater knows you're here. He saw your car in the basement on his way in. Sorry, I tried but he wouldn't be put off. He's on his way down."

"Damn it," Nathan said, jumping to his feet. He briefly considered making a beeline for the lift, but realised hiding would just delay the inevitable. Nathan grimaced and started clearing his desktop of the confidential documents he'd been working on.

"I suppose you'd better let him in then Sheryl. Oh, and make us a pot of coffee would you please."

A few minutes later the door to his office opened and Slater marched in. Slater, dressed in his expensive pinstriped suit, also wore an incredibly po-faced expression. Sheryl followed Slater carrying a silver tray holding coffee, milk, sugar, and two china cups. She gave her boss a wry smile and left the tray on the edge of Nathan's desk before leaving the two men alone.

"Peter, would you like some coffee?" Nathan gestured towards one of the leather chairs opposite his desk. "Please have a seat."

Slater remained standing, waving the coffee away, "You've no doubt heard your son assaulted Rod Jackson while escaping today. Rod's in hospital with a broken cheek, a broken nose, whiplash, four broken teeth and severe concussion."

"Yes. I just heard the news report a few minutes ago. I'm so sorry. Is Rod going to be okay?"

"Doctors say it could be a couple of days before he's out of hospital. After that, he'll need cosmetic surgery to repair his face. Guess whose bill we'll be putting that on?"

Williamson groaned inwardly and his shoulder slumped. "Okay, just let me know what the damage is and I'll sort it out as soon as I can."

"Damn right you will."

Slater turned to leave. "Oh and by the way," he said over his shoulder, "your son's a fucking nut bar."

Nathan watched Slater's back as he disappeared through the doorway.

*Tell me something I don't know already!*

Moments later Sheryl popped in and told him there were two detectives waiting to see him. "They won't say what it's about."

"That's okay. I've been expecting them. Send them in if you would please Sheryl. Oh and we'll need another cup."

Nathan felt exhausted already.

*Bloody Gerard!*

**********

The afternoon had turned into a scorcher. What little cloud had been around earlier that morning had long gone. Sweat dripped from Gerard's forehead as he stepped through the door.

He found the apartment just as he'd left it. A mustiness, caused by the place being unoccupied for much of the time, filled his nostrils. Pleased to be out of the sun, Gerard opened a window wide to let in some fresh air and then looked around.

The small utilitarian apartment had a double bed and chest of drawers tucked into an alcove off the main room. A modest kitchenette and tiny bathroom were the only other rooms in the place. The bathroom had a shower over a yellow stained bath, and linoleum that had seen better days. Still, Gerard didn't need flash. He needed private. He needed a place to hide and plan his next move.

Automatic payments and direct debits from a bank account opened under a false name, enabled Gerard to pay his rent and utilities without the need for personal contact. Whenever he had some spare cash, Gerard would deposit it into the secret account. A Post Office box, cleared once or twice a month handled his mail. Not that he got much apart from a few bank statements, a motorbike registration renewal notice once a year, and the odd advertising flyer that slipped through the 'no junk mail' request he'd made when initially renting the box.

The fake I.D. he'd needed to open the bank account had cost him more than the new 250cc motorcycle he kept in his storage locker down in the garage. Good quality forgeries were hard to obtain. Apart from setting up the bank account, buying the motorcycle, and renting the apartment, Gerard never used his fake I.D. for anything. It was strictly for emergencies only. Times like now.

The I.D. consisted of a New Zealand passport, and matching driver's licence. A change of hair colour and liberal application of instant-tanning liquid before the photos were taken had altered his appearance significantly. He also had a pair of dark-framed glasses he could wear whenever he went out.

Moving into the alcove, Gerard opened the top right hand dresser drawer and looked down at the fifty thousand dollars he'd stashed the day before his arrest. The cops had tried everything they could to trick and pressure him into revealing the money's location, but he'd remained silent, refusing to tell

AISES encourages students to seek summer internships for research or work experience and serves as a clearinghouse to match students with internship opportunities. College students also receive financial support through the college scholarship program, administered by AISES. To date over $8.7 million in scholarships have been awarded to nearly 5,000 students.

The development of future leaders is a priority for AISES. Our college students have opportunities to serve as leaders in their college chapters and also at the regional and national levels. Each of the seven AISES regions has a Regional Representative, a college student elected by his or her peers, who serves as liaison between the students of the region and the national organization. In addition, two college students, elected by students from across the country, serve as non-voting representatives of student interests on the AISES Board of Directors. Each year in February or March AISES hosts the Leadership Summit, attended by AISES student leaders and AISES professionals (Figure 4). The Leadership Summit provides workshops on career development and on leadership and matches students with professional mentors.

*Figure 4. Attendees at the 2013 AISES Leadership Summit, Santa Ana Pueblo. (Courtesy of AISES.)*

**Professional Programs: Leadership and Change**

Professionals at all levels, early career, mid-career, and executive level, benefit from engagement through AISES in networking, professional development, and giving back (http://www.aises.org/programs/professional). Professional development workshops are offered at the National Conference and at the Leadership Summit. For instance, one time in the past few years the ACS short course on Leading Change was offered in conjunction with an AISES National Conference. AISES professional members build networks with other the police anything except his name, address, and occupation. Gerard's silence had paid off. Now at least, he had a safe haven as well as some operating capital. Gerard would need both if he wanted to continue hunting.

When Gerard left the apartment at 4:00 p.m. he walked down to his storage locker grabbed the crash helmet and gloves off the shelf, and wheeled out the motorcycle. The helmet would further hide his identity, enabling him to move freely about the city. A bike was the obvious choice for day to day transport. Lot of easy parking would be available and, in the unlikely event he was spotted by the police, he could go places on a bike no cop driving a car would be able to follow, especially in the narrow streets of Wellington.

Gerard would need another van before he could hunt again. The police had impounded the last one. Still, the bike was fine most of the time. In fact it was perfect for the next job he had to do, one he'd been looking forward to for quite some time.

Gerard smiled as the bike started second kick. He rode out of the garage and turned right down the hill towards town. Once at the shoreline, Gerard took a left onto Oriental Parade and followed the harbour around past the town hall before making another left towards Lambton Quay and his father's office building.

**********

After locking his office, Nathan approached the lifts. It had been a shit of a day. The police had been at him for hours. "When was the last time you saw Gerard? Where did Gerard like to hang out? When did you last speak to your son? Who are his friends? Why are you paying for Gerard's defence? Where do you think he's gone? Has Gerard been in contact with you?"

*As If I'd protect that sadistic shit!*

Nathan felt a tension in his shoulders and a throbbing behind his eyes as he asked himself why the police refused to believe him when he said he wanted Gerard behind bars just as much as they did, or why they felt the need to go over the whole Bourne case again. Police had asked countless questions, and after he'd answered them, they'd started all over again. By the time the police had finished, he was not only losing his patience, he was absolutely knackered. With his mouth dryer than Central Otago in the summertime, Nathan couldn't wait to get home and pour a couple of large gin and tonics down his throat.

When the lift opened in the basement, Nathan walked swiftly towards his car. Pushing the button on his key, he heard a bleep as his car doors unlocked. As he reached for the door handle, footsteps sounded behind him.

"Who's that?" Nathan asked, turning his head toward to source of the noise. A blur raced towards his head, stars flashed and Nathan felt himself falling.

When Nathan opened his eyes he winced. The light made his head hurt. He tried to lift a hand to shield his eyes, then realised his hands were taped together. As the conga drums playing inside his skull subsided, his vision gradually cleared.

Gerard stood above him with a weird grin on his face. He held what looked like a pair of pliers in his hand. After a quick glance around, Nathan realised he was lying in the boot of a car, possibly his own, but he wasn't sure. He tried to sit upright but the lack of space and the tape around his arms and legs allowed him little movement. Gerard's hand pushed him back down.

Nathan tried to call out, but the duct tape Gerard had wrapped around his father's head, held his lips firm.

Gerard enjoyed the fear in his father's eyes. "Try to fuck me over, you pompous old bastard!" He reached down and grabbed his father's bound wrists. As he lifted them, Gerard clamped the secateurs onto one of his father's fingers.

Nathans eyes went wild with fear.

As Gerard squeezed hard, he heard a satisfying crunch as the finger came off at the second knuckle. Blood spurted from the stump as the finger dropped into Nathan's lap.

Gerard smiled.

*That felt so good.*

As Nathan screamed beneath the tape, Gerard shivered in delight.

"No point trying to yell. No one can hear you."

Breathing quick through his nose, Nathan scrunched his eyes together and gritted his teeth. A burning pain pulsated up his arm, and sweat poured off his face. As Gerard lifted his hands again, Nathan's mind reeled in horror.

With a snap, Nathan's ring finger came off. Ten seconds later the pinkie followed. Nathan's hand, wrist, and arm were on fire as the secateurs cut through sinew, flesh and bone. Twisting, trying to pull his hands away from Gerard's grasp, Nathan fought for his life. But Gerard was too strong. When another searing pain shot up his arm, Nathan's vision blurred and he felt the blackness close in around him. This time Nathan had no option, he surrendered to the dark.

Gerard made quick work of the fingers on the other hand, leaving the middle finger intact. This would be his special 'fuck you' message for the cops. Gerard could just imagine the cops finding his message. It was all such fun.

As Nathan lay quietly in the gathering pool of red, Gerard collected each bloody finger in turn and popped them into a jar before putting the jar into a jacket pocket. Then Gerard put some tape over his father's nose blocking off any remaining air supply. In a last act of defiance, Gerard wiped the blood from his hands onto his father's two thousand dollar suit. He took one last look at his father's body.

"Not such a big man now, are you?"

After making a final adjustment to his father's middle finger, Gerard closed the boot and smiled, satisfied with his afternoon's effort.

*Just a quick stop on the way home, and my work for the day is done.*

# CHAPTER 4 - TUESDAY MORNING

When Blondie arrived home from work after a long hard shift, her neck and back ached from sitting at her computer reviewing files for most of the day. She needed to immerse her weary body under a steady stream of hot water and work out the kinks. The house was silent. Blondie, suspecting her flatmate was still at work, went to her bedroom and stripped off her clothes.

Her pale skin glistened in the soft light that filtered through the fronds of the tree fern growing outside her bedroom window. She looked at her reflection in the mirror of the antique oak wardrobe standing in the corner of the room. Strong shoulders, angling down to a slim waist and softly rounded hips, gave her firm and well toned body a pleasing shape. Blondie reached up, cupping a breast in each hand, feeling their weight and shape.

*Not bad I suppose for someone my age.*

Blondie wrapped herself in a towel, and walked down the hallway toward the bathroom. The bathroom tiles were cool on her feet as she reached into the shower and turned on the taps. After letting the water run for a moment, she threw the towel over a hook on the wall, pulled back the shower curtain, and stepped under the water's invigorating warmth.

She began soaping herself, starting with her calves and thighs. As she moved up she let her hand linger in the small patch of soft hair between her legs and thought about the night she'd spent with her lover a few days previously. Closing her eyes Blondie imagined him in the shower with her. An almost inaudible sigh escaped her lips as the fantasy took hold. With her eyes closed and her hands moving over her body, she could almost feel him there with her.

Then the bathroom door opened.

"Who the hell is that?" Blondie said.

She knew her flatmate would have knocked. Blondie was about to yell out again, when the shower curtain slid back, revealing not her flatmate, but her lover. He was naked, and stood looking at her with desire obvious, both in his eyes and his body. Without saying a word his hand moved forward and cupped her breast, his thumb rotating around her hardening nipple. A familiar tingle of warmth filled her. Reaching out, she grabbed his forearms and pulled him gently into the shower. She felt his other hand slide down her belly and find the damp cleft between her legs, his gentle fingers sending ripples of pleasure through her. She pressed herself into his hand and slowly started stroking him too, moving her hand up and down his ...

Beep! Beep! Beep!

Blondie was startled out of her dream by the sound of the alarm going off.

*Damn, what was that all about? I don't even have a lover.*

She threw back the blanket as a bead of sweat cut a track down her temple and onto her pillow.

*Phew! Is it horny in here or is it just me?*

Rolling onto her side, Blondie looked through the shadows at the clock on the bedside table. It was 6:30 a.m., time for her to get ready for work.

*Damn alarm! Another half hours' sleep would have been so much more satisfying.*

**********

Chris and Andy met at the station ready to start work. They'd picked up the keys for an unmarked car, and were heading towards the door that lead downstairs to the parking garage when an officer behind the main desk called out.

"Hey guys, wait a minute. There's a delivery here for you."

Andy wandered over and took the courier envelope from the officer's hand. "Thanks Jim." Andy turned the envelope over. "Hmm ... I wonder who this is from."

"Come on!" Chris grumbled, "You can look at it in the car. We need to get moving."

Chris was never at his best until he had at least two cups of coffee in him.

Today they planned to catch up with Matu, one of their informants. Their relationship with Matu was simple. Matu told them what he knew, and they didn't bust him for possession of the marijuana he inevitably had on him.

"Let's hope Matu's got some information on that new dealer," Chris said as he jumped behind the wheel of the unmarked car.

The lead had come from a taxi-driver friend who'd overheard some inebriated passengers whispering about buying drugs late one night. The driver couldn't tell Chris and Andy very much apart from the name of the club his passengers had come out of, and that he'd dropped them at the railway station.

It wasn't much to go on, and the info didn't give any indication as to who the dealer was, but the two detectives hoped Matu might shed some light on the subject. If not they would have to stake out the club for a few days while they figured out who the dealer was. It would take longer, but they'd get there eventually.

This approach had worked before. They'd watch for a guy who dressed like a rock star, and had an entourage of women. That might be him. On the other hand, maybe he'd be the guy who drove the new sports car parked near the club, or the guy with the expensive clothes and heavy gold chains.

It always amazed Chris how compelled these guys were to flash their cash around. Did these dealers think, what's the use of having all this money if I can't buy a new car or impress the ladies with it?

The aspiring drug lords never realized the risk they ran flashing too much money about. Such overt behaviour was like waving a red flag with big yellow letters saying 'ARREST ME' on it to those whose job it was to ferret them out. Not that Chris or Andy complained about such stupidity. It made their job a lot easier. By the time some dealers realised their mistake, it was too late. They'd be in jail doing three years for supply, and trying desperately to preserve their virginity.

Usually, Chris and Andy told people they arrested a few jail-time horror stories. These tales of prison brutality, combined with some not so gentle persuasion, frightened many small time dealers into informing on some of the big fish further up the supply line. The importers and manufacturers were the ones the two detectives really wanted. The bigger the fish, the better Andy and Chris liked catching them.

As Chris pulled out of the garage, Andy turned the parcel over in his hands, feeling its weight and shape, trying to guess what was inside.

"How'd the date go last night Andy? Was she as cute as her picture?"

"She was nice, just not my cuppa tea. No chemistry. You know pretty soon if it's not going anywhere. This one kept talking about bloody astrology all the time. God I hate all that 'what's your sign' shit. Like duh ... as if the stars and planets could possibly affect our lives. Did you know that bus over there has more gravitational effect on us than Venus?"

"Hey don't be so hasty. I once had an Aunty who swore by it. After doing her chart, her astrologer told her she was going on a trip to somewhere hot. She died a few days later of a heart attack. She was an evil cow who deserved to burn in hell, so who knows, maybe there's something to it after all."

Andy chuckled. "You are a warped and twisted individual Detective Spacey, but I like the way you think."

As they drove along Courtenay Place, curiosity got the best of him and Andy tore the courier pack open, tipping the contents into his lap.

Chris heard a sharp intake of breath.

"Oh fuck!"

The shocked tone of Andy's voice snapped Chris's head around. What he saw made him swerve the car to the curb.

The two men stared at the chilli jar sitting in Andy's lap.

"Jesus Christ!" Chris said. "Are those what I think they are?"

**********

Warner sat at his desk, going over the details of the Nathan Williamson interview and reviewing files from the archives when the phone on his desk rang.

"Warner."

"Hey boss, guess what. Your favourite prison escapee just sent

Chris and Andy a jar of fingers."

"Oh shit. Not another child is it?"

As soon as he'd asked the question, Warner wasn't so sure he wanted Blondie to tell him the answer.

"Adult fingers they reckon. Still it must be Williamson eh? I mean, who else is crazy enough to do that?"

"So where are they? The fingers I mean."

"The guys are near Courtenay Place. They're on their way back to the station with them now."

"Okay. I'll go and meet them downstairs. Get forensics on standby and tell them we'll need to run some prints pronto."

"Okay boss. I'm on to it. See you in a few minutes."

As Andy and Chris drove down the ramp into the parking garage under the station, they noticed a group of constables standing around one of the cars. One was miming the act of chopping a finger off and acting the goat. The jungle drums were already beating.

Chris noticed the eyes of the group follow them as they walked past, and heard the stifled laugh from one of the younger officers. Ignoring them, he swiped his I.D. card through the slot and pushed the station's back door open.

Up a flight of steps, and down a narrow corridor they came to the main office where Warner greeted them as they came through the door.

"Hey you two, we need to have a chat about this new development. Come up to my office once you're done here. Okay?"

"Yes sir," Andy said in a serious tone as he delicately held the courier envelope between two fingers at arm's length. "We'll just get the chain of evidence sorted for these … um … fingers and be right up."

As Warner headed back upstairs, Andy placed the parcel gently on the counter.

"So those are the fingers eh?" The sergeant asked, bending down and twisting his neck sideways trying to get a look inside.

Andy nodded.

The Sergeant picked up the phone and made a call to

forensics.

Forensics would attempt to identify the victim and also check the jar and envelope for prints or any other clues useful in proving who had sent the courier pack.

After a brief conversation, the Sergeant hung up and then grabbed a couple of sheets of paper from under the counter. "They're on the way down. In the meantime, here are the forms you'll need to fill out."

A few minutes later, a technician wearing gloves and carrying a plastic bag arrived. Once the chain of evidence forms were completed, and signed by all parties, Andy and Chris were free to go upstairs for their meeting with Warner. After a quick thanks to the Sergeant, they left to catch the lift to the fourth floor.

"Chris, Andy, you remember Detective Green," Warner said as the two detectives entered, nodding his head in Blondie's direction.

Chris smiled and extended his hand. Blondie's skin was soft and warm, her handshake firm. "Hi Blondie."

When Blondie looked up at Chris, she felt a warm sensation course through her. It was the eyes that first attracted her to a man. His were so pale and piercing, she stood mesmerised. Although she'd seen Chris around the station a few times, she'd never seen him up close and personal like this before. Remembering the dream she'd had that morning, she wondered if it was an omen.

When she realised she was still holding Chris's hand, Blondie blushed.

"And this is Andy," Chris said smiling, nodding in Andy's direction.

"Hi Andy," Blondie said, quickly shaking his hand before sitting down.

Blondie thought Andy looked a bit pale as he fidgeted from foot to foot. She knew she had that effect on some men, but then figured it was more likely to be the after affects of the shock he'd got when opening the parcel of fingers.

"Pull up a chair guys," Warner said, pointing towards a row

of chairs lined up against the far wall of his office. "Let's see if we can figure out what Williamson's playing at."

Both men dragged a chair over to Warner's desk and sat beside Blondie who'd opened her laptop ready to take notes.

"You guys seem to be Williamson's flavour of the month for some reason. Any idea why he'd want to send you fingers?" Warner asked.

"Apart from our involvement in the Bourne case, I can't think of a reason." Chris replied. "We've had no prior contact."

"Williamson must have read the arrest report. That would have had our names on it," Andy said. "I had a word with one of the detectives that went to the prison after the escape. He told me the lawyer's briefcase is missing."

"It was." Warner confirmed.

"That would explain it then." Chris said.

Warner leaned back in his chair. "So Gerard's just playing mind games again?"

Chris nodded. "He must be. Nothing else makes sense."

"Well whatever his reason, let's hope he's given us a few clues this time." Warner said before looking towards Blondie. "How long do you think forensics will take?"

"Once they print the severed fingers, not long. All up maybe an hour max assuming the victim is in the system. I made a couple of quick calls to the local hospitals. Nobody with missing fingers has turned up in the Emergency Department."

"Okay, so the victim is still out there somewhere." Warner looked towards Chris and Andy. "Anything else you can add to the puzzle?"

"I noticed he's still using the same jars." Andy said.

"Yeah, I wonder what that's all about."

While the four of them discussed the case a few moments longer, trying to come up with something that might help lead them to Williamson, Chris noticed Blondie sneak a quick glance in his direction a couple of times. She was also fiddling with her hair. He'd been around long enough to know signs of interest when he saw them.

Chris was interested too. Blondie had beautiful clear skin, and sexy brown eyes that drew him in. It had been a while since he'd been involved with a woman, especially one as gorgeous as Blondie. Butterflies did a quick lap of his stomach.

Chris hadn't dated much recently. There just hadn't been anyone that grabbed his interest. Why he'd become so particular of late he wasn't quite sure. He wasn't a prude, but then he wasn't a player either. Sure, he'd had the odd fling, but nothing had stuck.

Warner and the three detectives threw ideas around for another ten minutes or so, but their speculation shed little light.

Warner slid back his chair and stood up. "Okay guys, thanks for your help. Blondie, let's go and see how forensics are doing." Warner handed Chris a business card. "Any more contact from Williamson and I want you to ring me, day or night. Blondie give him your card too, just in case my cell's out of range."

Despite her reservations about dating colleagues, Blondie jotted her home phone number on her card before she handed it to Chris, hoping he'd take the hint and call her sometime. As Chris took her card, he looked straight into Blondie's eyes and smiled. He noticed a faint blush appear on her cheeks again. Glancing down at the card, he noticed the extra number below her normal contact details. His smile widened as the butterflies did a few more laps.

Blondie hoped like hell Chris didn't think she was being too obvious. A little forwardness could be sexy, but seeming desperate was anything but.

As Chris and Andy followed Blondie out of the office towards the lift, Chris couldn't help notice her lovely curves. Reaching into his jacket pocket, he fiddled with the card she'd given him and smiled.

*This might be my lucky day.*

**********

After an early breakfast of black coffee and two slices of toast, covered with a thick spread of marmite, Gerard cut his hair using a pair of scissors and a shaving mirror. Then he applied some of the hair dye left over from when he'd got his false I.D. photographs taken. After letting the dye take for a few minutes, he showered, had a shave, and got dressed.

His costume consisted of black Levi jeans, charcoal tee shirt, black leather bomber jacket and black boots. After a quick rummage through a kitchen drawer he found the pair of dark-framed glasses he'd used as part of his disguise on previous occasions and gave them a quick wipe on his t-shirt before putting them on. Now, according to his false driver's license, the person looking back at him from the mirror was Tom Renfrew, organ donor.

Amazed at the difference a new hairstyle, glasses, and a few clothes could make, Gerard struck a pose, and then laughed at his reflection. He figured this new look would fool all but those who knew him well, and they, as his father had so recently discovered, were becoming an endangered species.

Today, Gerard wanted to beat the rush and hit the car yards when they opened. Now that his father was out of the way, it was time to buy a van. He had specific requirements which might take a while to find, so the sooner he got moving the better. Going to the dresser Gerard took twenty thousand dollars in cash from the top drawer and zipped it into the pocket of his jacket.

*Thank you Mr and Mrs Bourne, this should cover it.*

Riding his motorbike down into town and then onto the motorway, Gerard cruised through the Terrace Tunnel, and then north along State Highway 1. After a few kilometres, he veered right and took the over-bridge which led to State Highway 2 and the motorway to the Hutt Valley.

Hills covered in regenerating native bush towered steeply up to Gerard's left. Off in the distance to his right, he could make out the old quarantine station on Somes Island. To the island's right, the interisland ferry was steaming its way into Wellington harbour. The ferry seemed on a collision course with the island, but Gerard knew it would soon turn to port and angle towards its berth just north of the big aluminium-sheathed sports stadium, nicknamed 'The Cake Tin' on the outskirts of the CBD.

Traffic going in his direction was light compared to the tangled mayhem that fought its way bumper to bumper into the city. As he drove further around the foreshore, the Hutt Valley appeared rising towards the Rimutaka Range in the distance.

The Hutt was a mixture of light industry, middle and low cost housing, with the odd pocket of luxury homes both on the valley floor and high on the hills above. It was also home to a quite a few second-hand car dealers. Gerard was confident he'd be able to find an appropriate van in one of them.

**********

After their meeting with Warner, Chris and Andy sat at their desks working on their incident reports. It was the part of their job the men liked the least. Chris turned Blondie's card over in his fingers as he pondered how best to word his statement. "Blondie's pretty hot don't you reckon?"

"She sure is," replied Andy. "I noticed the way she was looking at you. You might have a fan there big guy."

"Did you? I hadn't noticed," Chris lied. "Warner seemed a bit tense. Poor guy's right back in the firing line. I hope they get a break and find that sicko. What a wanker sending us a jar of fingers like that."

"Not wrong there pal," Andy agreed. "It's put me right off jalapeños."

**********

Forensics, situated in the back of the building on the second floor, was a small operation, but they got the job done. If testing exceeded their capabilities, items would be sent to the Auckland lab or one of the scientific organisations that worked in conjunction with the police on a case-by-case basis.

By the time Warner and Blondie approached the counter that divided the lab from the office, the young technician had taken prints from the fingers and sat drinking his morning coffee as the computer ran a comparison search using A.F.I.S. (Automatic

Fingerprint Information Service). His colleague testing the courier envelope further back in the lab looked up as they entered.

"Hi, you must be D.I. Warner and Detective Green," the young man behind the computer said. "I heard you were on the way down."

"Yes I'm Warner, and this is Detective Green. Any idea how much longer it will be before you know something?"

The technician got up from his chair and approached them giving Blondie a quick once-over before turning back towards Warner. "The search should be finished in fifteen minutes or so. We're into the last quarter of the database now. If something's going to turn up, it'd better be soon."

As Warner and Blondie discussed getting a quick cup of coffee, the computer started beeping, and the word 'match' flashed on its monitor.

"Looks like we've just hit the jackpot," Blondie said smiling.

Warner and Blondie went around the counter and followed the technician over towards the screen. As he sat down at the screen, they peered over his shoulders. The technician pressed a button on the keyboard then read the results aloud. "It says here the prints belong to a Nathan Harmon Williamson. You know who that is?"

Warner nodded. "Yeah we know him all right. His son's the guy who escaped from prison yesterday."

"Now all we need to do is find the rest of him," added Blondie.

"Hope he doesn't need to use the yellow pages," the technician smirked.

"Very droll," Warner said. "Did you get anything useful from the courier pack or the jar?"

"It's just a standard courier pack, available from any Post Shop. The tracking number originated from Manners Street if that helps." The technician nodded towards the back of the lab. "My colleague is checking it now. We'll run the prints he finds next. Then we'll do the same on the jar. Might take a while, but we'll let you know if anything interesting turns up."

"Looks like twelve prints on the envelope," the other technician said walking towards them. "Give me another fifteen minutes and we should be able to start searching."

Warner gave them a thumbs-up. "Okay, guys. Well done."

"Yeah thanks," Blondie said before following Warner out of forensics back to the lifts. "So boss, where do you want to start looking for Nathan Williamson, home or office?"

"His interview yesterday didn't finish until nearly five o'clock. Let's have a quick look at his office first. We can send a couple of officers to check his home. I doubt he's alive knowing Gerard, but then stranger things have happened."

"I'll give dispatch a call, see who they've got free at the moment," Blondie said opening her cell.

"Okay. While you do that I'll just pop upstairs a moment."

While Warner was upstairs, Blondie arranged for two detectives to go to the home address of Nathan Williamson. When Warner returned a few minutes later jangling a set of car keys in his hand, Blondie opened her notebook and gave Warner the address of Nathan Williamson's office.

"Shit, it's only around the corner. I could have saved myself a trip. Let's just walk it. You know what trying to park on Lambton Quay is like this time of day."

Seven minutes later, they were outside a sixteen story retail and office complex that went up just prior to the 1987 crash. Like many buildings constructed in those heady days, it's façade of tinted glass and grand foyer were designed to impress. In the foyer, polished brass and marble tiles covered every surface. Small niches, each with a decorative urn and illuminated by spotlights inset in the ceiling high above, lined the walls on both sides. A brass-framed directory mounted on one wall showed the names of the tenants. After finding Williamson's name, they walked towards the lift.

Although much smaller, the style of the 8th floor lobby replicated that of the main foyer downstairs. Six office suites led off it, each with its own ornate door complete with gold lettering. Entering the door for 'Williamson Mortgage Brokers', they found themselves in a nicely appointed outer office with quality prints in expensive frames hanging on the walls. Two leather reception chairs and a small coffee table loaded with magazines sat against the wall on the left. The furniture was classy, but not ostentatious, the room impressive, but tasteful.

"I see Williamson's a fan of the Impressionists." Warner said, noticing a large print depicting a field of colourful flowers on the right hand wall.

"Or the interior decorator was," Blondie said. "Looks like Monet."

"I think you're right. Did you see that Monet exhibition at Te Papa a couple of years ago? It was amazing. My wife dragged me along, but then I got so engrossed, she had to drag me away."

"Yes I went twice. The one of Notre Dame was my favourite. It didn't look like much up close, but from a distance it looked like a photograph. How the hell did he do that?"

The woman behind the reception desk looked up from her paperwork as they approached.

"Hello, I'm Detective Inspector Warner and this is my colleague Detective Green, we're with the Wellington police," Warner said, holding up his identity card.

Warner gave the woman a cursory once over. She was in her mid-forties, reasonably attractive with blond hair and a minimum of make-up. She wore a dark skirt and white blouse. A braided cord with a piece of polished paua-shell hung around her neck above an ample bosom.

"What can I do for you Officers?" She asked, smiling up at them with perfect white teeth.

"We're looking for Nathan Williamson," replied Warner.

"I'm sorry, he isn't here yet. May I ask the nature of your enquiry?"

"When was the last time you saw him?" Warner said, ignoring her question.

"Let's see ... it was just before I left to go home yesterday afternoon about five. Why?" She asked a little anxiously.

"We need to find him. Are you Williamson's only employee?

"Yes," she replied. "There's just the two of us in the office. I've worked here about two years. Is everything okay?"

"We're not sure Miss um ...?"

"Crawford, Sheryl Crawford. What's going on? Has something happened to Nathan?"

"We suspect he's been involved in an incident." Blondie said.

"An incident? Oh dear, you don't mean he's been hurt do you?"

"Look, I'm sorry Miss Crawford, but I can't really say much until we've had a chance to complete our investigation."

"Oh dear," Sheryl repeated, her face dropping any hint of the smile.

Blondie looked towards the door behind Sheryl and asked. "Have you been in his office today?"

"Yes I got in about eight o'clock to do some typing before Nathan arrived. Nathan usually comes in about nine," Sheryl said, her voice a little shaky. "His car was in the basement when I arrived, so I thought he'd come in early too ... but when I got up here there was no sign of him. I figured he'd just gone to get coffee or breakfast maybe, but he's missed a few appointments ... most unlike him. Oh dear, I hope he's okay."

"Did you try him on his cell phone?" Blondie asked.

"Yes but there was no answer, I left him a message but haven't heard back."

"What type of car does he drive Miss Crawford?" Warner asked.

"A BMW, it's parked in number 23 down in the basement."

"Okay. Do you mind if I have a quick look in his office while we're here? We need to eliminate the obvious."

Sheryl shrugged and made a sweeping gesture with her arm that seemed to say 'go see for yourself if you don't believe me'.

In the inner office Warner saw no sign of a disturbance. Everything appeared to be in its proper place. The office was of reasonable size. A solid oak pedestal desk sat in its centre, with a brown leather swivel chair behind it. Two matching straight-backed chairs were in front of the desk, their backs to the door. To the left, bookcases filled the wall. Another Monet print, this one of an arched bridge over a lily pond, hung on the wall opposite the bookcase. Covering the wall behind the desk were framed certificates and photographs. The room was comfortable, warm, and inviting.

Warner walked behind the desk and looked at a few of the photographs. They showed Williamson with a variety of politicians and celebrities. One showed him shaking hands with the current Minister of Finance, albeit much younger in the photo than he was today. Another showed him sitting at a dinner table with a group of high-profile businessmen.

Warner turned slowly and scanned the office. There was no obvious blood, and as Sheryl had said, no Nathan. No mutilation had taken place here.

As Warner re-entered the main office, he looked towards Blondie who'd been chatting with the receptionist. "I'll go down and take a quick look at Nathan's car while you finish taking Miss Crawford's statement."

Blondie nodded at Warner as he walked off towards the lift.

"I hope Nathan calls soon," Sheryl said.

"Me too," Blondie said knowing how unlikely that was. Even if by some miracle Nathan were alive, he certainly wouldn't be pushing the buttons on a phone any time soon.

On his arrival in the basement, Warner walked down the left-hand side of the garage towards number 23. The car park had a low ceiling and was poorly lit. It smelled of damp. The heels of his shoes created an echo as the sound of each step rebounded off the concrete walls.

There was a faint but familiar odour as he neared the car. Not strong, but Warner recognised the smell. He could see nothing out of the ordinary through the windows so he went around towards the rear. Splatters of blood on the back of the BMW, and brownish drops on the concrete floor strengthened his suspicions of what he'd find inside the car's boot. He called Blondie on his cell phone and let her know what he'd discovered.

"I'm almost done here, nothing new from Sheryl unfortunately. I may as well come down."

"Okay, but make sure Sheryl stays in the office. I have a feeling this isn't going to be pretty."

Blondie closed her phone and looked at Sheryl. "Would you

please stay here by the phone while I go down and meet my colleague? I shouldn't be too long."

Sheryl reached into a drawer and rummaged around. "Here, you may need these."

Warner greeted Blondie when she arrived in the basement a few minutes later. "I'll go organise a warrant so we can search the car." he said. "Stay here and keep the scene secure, I'll be back as soon as I can."

"No need," interjected Blondie, tossing a set of car-keys towards Warner. "His secretary had them. It's a company car. She's given us permission to have a look."

"Let's see what we've got then."

As Warner slotted the key into the lock, the faint but unmistakable sound of a cell phone ringing, came from within.

"I'll bet you ten bucks that's Sheryl," Blondie said.

As suspected, Williamson's body was inside. He was, without any doubt, deceased. The smell was stronger now, overpowering in fact. Williamson had soiled himself either during the attack or shortly after death once his muscles had relaxed. The middle finger of Williamson's otherwise fingerless hand, raised in a 'fuck you' salute, looked odd, but they both got the message loud and clear.

"Cheeky prick," Warner said. "Fuck you too Gerard!"

"Pity we didn't keep Nathan Williamson under surveillance after his interview, eh boss?"

"No reason for us to suspect Nathan was in danger. He was paying for Gerard's defence after all. Why would Gerard want to kill him?"

"Apart from being crazy you mean?"

"Unfortunately poor old Nathan won't be giving us the answer."

"Unless you know a good clairvoyant."

"I'll leave the mumbo jumbo to the TV detectives," Warner said, pulling his cell phone out his pocket. "It's time to get the Crime Scene people on the move."

The pathologist and two technical boffins arrived twenty minutes later. Elizabeth Rhodes was well known to both Blondie and Warner. She was a no-nonsense sort of woman. With a quick nod to them, she went straight to work. Fifteen minutes later she had finished and walked over to where Warner and Blondie were standing a few metres away.

"From the body's temperature, I'd estimate time of death at between five and seven p.m. yesterday. He may have bled out, but seeing his airways are blocked I suspect the cause of death will be asphyxiation. The autopsy will tell the whole story."

"Okay, thanks Liz." Warner said. "Ring me if you discover anything new."

Elizabeth nodded. "You'll be the first to know."

As Elizabeth packed up her gear, Blondie stepped closer to Warner. "Gerard certainly didn't waste any time."

Warner shook his head in disgust. "And here I was hoping the bastard might lay low for awhile, give us a chance to find him before he went psycho on us again."

As Elizabeth left the garage, the crime scene guys got to work. They were both around six feet tall, wore dark blue trousers, light blue shirts and lightweight blue jackets.

The senior technician introduced himself as Bill Moananui. "And this is my colleague Paul MacDonald, but everyone calls him Mac."

"I might stick around. At the moment we've got nothing to go on so anything you can tell me will be a help."

"Sure Detective Inspector," Bill said. "We'll get stuck in then."

Bill had the build of a rugby prop, a wide easy smile, dark hair and brown eyes. Paul was just the opposite, with light hair, the lean body of a tennis player, and an exasperated expression that gave the impression he carried the weight of the world on his shoulders.

Both men carried black equipment cases. They donned their latex gloves and white overalls, and went about their business with unemotional efficiency. They'd seen it all before. As cases went, this wasn't nearly as bad as some they'd encountered. One 'P' addict the previous year had hacked two people to death with a machete. They'd been assigned to pick up the pieces, literally. The murders had made the front page of the paper. 'Rwanda

Style Killings in New Zealand', the headlines had said. But dead children were the worst. No matter how long you'd been on the job, the death of a child was always hard to deal with.

As Bill and Mac got to work, Warner turned to Blondie. "I want you to go back upstairs and tell Sheryl she needs to update her C.V. I'm not very good at that sort of thing. In the meantime I'll organise a couple of detectives to canvas the other offices in the building. You never know, one of the tenants might have seen something."

After Blondie informed Sheryl of the demise of her former employer, Sheryl sat there stunned, tears streaming down her face, staring into the distance.

"Sheryl, can you help me please? I'm sorry, I know this is hard for you," Blondie said softly a few minutes later. "Do you know Nathan's son Gerard? He's our main suspect. Any information you can give us about him would be a big help."

"You think Gerard did this?"

"It seems likely. Police arrested Gerard last Wednesday for the kidnapping and mutilation of Leonard Bourne. You know, the kid who had his fingers cut off."

"Arrested last Wednesday? How could he have killed Nathan if he's been arrested?"

"You obviously haven't seen the news. Gerard escaped from custody yesterday morning. Nathan had his fingers removed, just like the Bourne kid. That's why we're confident Gerard killed his father."

"Had his fingers removed? You mean like chopped off? Oh my god ..." Sheryl put a hand to her mouth, and continued sobbing. A few minutes later she blew her nose and looked up at Blondie with bloodshot eyes. "The only time Nathan mentioned Gerard recently, was to say he'd organized Mr Jackson from the law firm upstairs to represent him. He never said ... never said anything about a kidnapping."

Blondie handed Sheryl another tissue. "Take your time."

Sheryl folded the tissue and blew her nose again before continuing. "I don't know why, but I just assumed it was some minor thing. Nathan didn't give me any details. Is that why the police were here to see Nathan yesterday?"

Blondie nodded. "Now think hard. Is that the only thing Nathan mentioned to you about Gerard? You can't remember anything else?"

"I don't think they got on. Nathan rarely mentioned his son, except to say what a pain in the arse he was. I think he asked for money a few times, but that was a while ago now." Another sob escaped Sheryl's lips.

Blondie tried to be as gentle with the secretary as she could while obtaining as much information as possible. She was just closing her notebook as Warner arrived back in the office.

"Lab boys are just finishing up. Nothing new to report until they run the prints they've found. Oh, and I've called the unit we sent to Williamson's home, and told them what we've found."

"Miss Crawford," Warner said. "I'd like to take a closer look around Nathan's office again if you don't mind." Without waiting for confirmation Warner headed into the inner office, only hearing a faint 'that's okay' from Sheryl after he'd passed through the door.

Warner picked up the diary on Nathan's desk and scanned back through the pages looking for any reference to Gerard. The only mention of Gerard he found was a brief note from the previous day which said, 'Jackson/Gerard 9:00 a.m.' The result of that meeting they knew already.

After a quick thumb through the pages, Warner soon realized there were no revelations to be gained from them. Searching the drawers of the desk, he found what one would expect to find in an office, but nothing to indicate the whereabouts of Gerard. Having read the police report written after the interview with Nathan Williamson's on the afternoon of his death, Warner was convinced Nathan knew nothing about his son's whereabouts.

*Damn you Gerard. Where the hell are you?*

Warner closed the diary and rejoined Blondie and Sheryl in the outer office.

"I suppose we'd better find Williamson's wife and tell her the bad news," Blondie said.

"They divorced years ago." Sheryl said. "She's moved to

Australia, Gympie or somewhere like that. They didn't get on. He rarely mentioned her name. He never told me why they split, and I didn't ask."

Sheryl's tears began to flow full force once again. She and Nathan had been lovers for over a year. They'd been in the process of planning an extended holiday in the Cayman Islands.

# CHAPTER 5 - TUESDAY AFTERNOON

Gerard visited four car yards before lunch. Then after grabbing a sandwich at one of the local shops he started looking again. He'd found two vans that were possibilities, but still wanted to check a couple more yards out before making a final decision. It wasn't until 2:00 p.m. that he found the right one—a white Toyota Hi-Ace, long wheelbase, petrol, five-speed automatic, complete with stereo—and it was white, the most common colour, which suited his purposes perfectly. Common was good, especially for someone who wanted to blend in.

The odometer only had 62,000 kilometres on the clock, and the price was within his range. The van had nothing to make it stand out from the thousands of others just like it roaming the city.

Being an ex delivery vehicle, a wire mesh screen dividing the cargo area from the two seats in front had been fitted to protect the driver from flying parcels in the event of a sudden stop or accident. The screen also made the van perfect for locking things in, an added bonus in Gerard's opinion. Apart from the screen, the back of the van was an empty space. With a few minor alterations, it would be perfect.

"Hi there, nice looking vehicle eh?" The salesman said as he approached Gerard. "Not a dent on her."

"How negotiable are you on price?"

"Will you be paying cash?"

"Yeah, but I've seen a couple other possibilities so what's the best deal you can do?"

"If you don't mind waiting a minute sir, I'll go and speak to my boss. I'm sure we can sort something out for you."

When the salesman came back to Gerard with a price that was almost a thousand dollars below the ticket price, and included a three-month mechanical warranty, Gerard told the salesman he'd take it.

"Come with me," the salesman said leading Gerard to his office.

Gerard paid cash, using the Roseneath address on the change

of ownership papers. Then getting the salesman to give him a hand, he loaded the motorbike into the back of the Toyota, and secured it in place with a length of rope.

"Thanks Mr Renfrew, by the way my name's Troy Simpson, if I can ever help you again with anything please give me a call." Troy handed Gerard a business card.

Gerard put the card in his pocket without reply and climbed into the van. Driving out of the lot, he turned left and drove to the nearest petrol station. There he filled the tank. As a precaution he checked the oil and water, and adjusted the tyre pressure. Then he drove back around the harbour towards his apartment, stopping once along the way to buy a few supplies and a copy of the *DomPost,* Wellington's daily newspaper.

Getting the bike out of the van was easy enough by himself. Gerard put it in neutral and rolled it out the back door, the wheels bouncing on the concrete floor of the garage as it dropped. After manoeuvring it back into the storage locker, he climbed the stairs back to his apartment.

Once inside, he sat down at the table, lit a cigarette, and opened the paper. The story of his escape was on page three. He read the whole story twice. The details were surprisingly accurate. Unlike his father, it seemed the lawyer would survive despite his beating. The picture of Gerard in the newspaper looked nothing at all like Tom Renfrew, and that pleased Gerard. There wasn't much chance of someone recognising him from that grainy old shot.

Satisfied, Gerard scanned the classified ads looking for a quiet little space he could rent. A small warehouse unit or workshop tucked away down a service lane or quiet dead end street. A place he could use as a storage room and more importantly, a play room. Privacy was paramount. He couldn't risk a location where someone might hear a child scream. He wouldn't be making that mistake again.

After circling a few possibilities, Gerard got up from the chair and stretched out on the bed. He'd look at them in the morning. Right now, he needed to do some serious thinking and have an afternoon snooze.

Exhausted from all the frenetic activity of the last couple days it wasn't long before he was asleep.

**********

By the time they'd finished their paperwork and eaten lunch, Chris and Andy only had three hours before their shift finished so they decided to drive down to Waitangi Park and try once more to find Matu.

The park was a people magnet in summer and one of Matu's favourite hangouts. On a nice day, both locals and tourists took full advantage of the large open space the inner city park provided. It was just a stroll down the road from Te Papa, one of the most popular tourist attractions in town.

Young people played Frisbee, or Hacky Sack, on the large grassy area in the park's centre. Skateboarders, and BMX riders, used the concrete ramps and jumps provided for that purpose on the southern side. Parents watched their children clamber over the gym equipment in the children's play area, chatting to each other as they kept an eye on their little ones, while other visitors to the park sat on the benches, or the grass, relaxing in the sun.

Before leaving the station, Andy put on some old gym clothes he kept in his locker so he could wander about undercover. He didn't look like a cop when dressed in his sports gear. Being short, he didn't fit the image most people had of policemen. TV stereotypes helped foster the myth of tall strapping coppers, and on more than one occasion, a dealer had made the mistake of offering Andy drugs. After this morning's finger episode, he almost felt like taking some.

Once they'd negotiated the traffic, the two detectives left their car near the marina and walked the rest of the way to the park. Their plan was a simple one. Andy would stroll around the park to see if he could find the informant, while Chris remained stationed at the western end in case Matu came in his direction. As Andy wandered down the northern side of the park, wearing a red bandana tied around his head, sunglasses, shorts, and a T-shirt, he blended right in. He strolled about as if he didn't have a care in the world, just another dude enjoying a summer's day.

After covering a hundred metres or so, a group of young men standing on the end of a small wooden pier that jutted out into the harbour caught Andy's attention. They were passing what he assumed to be a joint, around in a circle. A couple of the guys glanced briefly in his direction, but didn't seem to care if Andy saw what they were doing or not. He didn't look a threat, especially as there were six of them, and only one of him.

Andy started walking towards the young men with the intention of giving them a warning, but when he noticed Matu's brightly coloured Rasta hat and long dreadlocks about a hundred metres off to his right, he veered in that direction instead.

Matu had been feeding them information for over a year now and had proven a useful source of information on the Wellington drug scene. The two detectives had first caught Matu in possession of marijuana almost three years ago, but rather than arrest him, they'd come to an arrangement. Most judges hated possession cases anyway, and besides, Matu was harmless. He lived on the street in the summer, sleeping rough, and used the Night Shelter in the wintertime. The detectives knew Matu covered the cost of his own marijuana use by selling small amounts, but he was such a small player he was far more valuable to them on the street.

Neither Chris nor Andy saw marijuana as a big deal. Plenty of people smoked it these days. Even a few policemen and women had a puff from time to time, not that they'd admit it. Both men held similar positions that marijuana should be legalised, or at the very least, decriminalised. That would free up police resources, take a big chunk out of the income gangs were raking in from its sale, and minimise the contact the average person had with the more harmful drugs that often ran in the same illegal circles. Police had far fewer problems with pot smokers than they did with the drunks, and 'P' users, both of which were far more likely to be violent or destructive.

"Hey there Matu," Andy said as he approached.

The informant glanced around, checking he couldn't be overheard. "Officer Andy, how's tricks?"

"Not bad, not bad. Hey, I don't suppose you've heard anything about some new dealer working out of The Cloud Nine Club?"

"Come to think of it, a mate did mention he'd scored down there the other night."

"Did your mate give you any details?"

Matu nodded. "A few. He said the guy's pakeha and has a ponytail … oh, and he mentioned he had some awesome looking tats. Funny, it used to be just us brown fellas wearing them, but nowadays everyone's inked up."

"You're not wrong there." Andy said before slipping Matu a bill from his pocket, "Thanks. If we find this guy, we'll put another gold star on your report card. If you hear anything else, you make sure you give me a ring okay?"

"No problem Officer Andy," Matu said, giving Andy the thumbs up.

After completing his loop of the park, Andy gave Chris the news. "It seems we're looking for a European guy with a ponytail and tats. That should narrow the field somewhat."

"So how was Matu?"

"He smelled of pot, but then that's pretty normal for Matu."

"True."

Andy hefted his gym bag over his shoulder. "Hey, seeing it's almost knock-off time. What say we finish early? I'm knackered."

Before Chris could reply, his cell phone rang interrupting their conversation. He pulled the phone from his pocket and flipped it open.

"Spacey."

"Hi, Chris."

"Hey Blondie."

"Just thought I'd let you know that those fingers you received this morning belonged to Williamson Senior."

"Gerard killed off his old man?"

"Looks that way. We found Nathan's body at work, stuffed in the boot of his car. No witnesses unfortunately, not that there's much doubt about who did it."

"Hey well thanks for the update. Good luck finding the

bastard."

"Thanks, I suspect we'll need it. Look, I'd better go. The press have arrived to interview Warner. Hope to see you around sometime."

"Sounds like a plan. Catch you soon detective."

Chris told Andy the news as they drove back to the station to drop off the car. It had been a strange day, one they'd remember for a while. As he drove, Chris prayed he'd be able to sleep that night. Maybe if he thought about Blondie, his bad dreams would disappear.

**********

Reporters, cameramen, and photographers jostled for position in the crowded conference room. An expectant buzz crackled through the room. The press conference had deliberately been scheduled early enough for the TV crews to make the 6:00 p.m. news if they hurried.

At five o'clock Warner walked into the conference room wearing an expression nearly as dark as his charcoal suit. He climbed two steps onto a slightly raised platform, and stood behind the dais. Warner switched on the microphone and tapped it softly to insure it was functioning properly. The reporters framed their pictures of him to include the New Zealand flags hanging limp and unmoving from the poles on either side of the dais.

Warner cleared his throat and the clamour ceased, as if by magic. After shuffling a few pages, the Detective Inspector read a prepared statement giving the basic facts of the murder in Lambton Quay. After finishing the statement Warner asked if there were any questions.

A host of reporters spoke at once. One from Radio New Zealand raised his voice above the others, catching Warner's attention.

"Do you think the murder of Nathan Williamson has anything to do with the escape of his son from prison yesterday?"

"Yes we believe the two events are connected. We are doing

our best to recapture Gerard Williamson so he can be questioned regarding his father's death," Warner replied.

"Is he the only suspect you have at this time?" A reporter from a local radio station asked.

"He is, but we'll know more once all the evidence has been analysed."

"Why would Gerard want to kill his father?"

"Sorry, I'm not prepared to speculate on that."

"Is it true the murdered man had his fingers chopped off?" Someone yelled out from the back.

"Until the autopsy has been completed, and family contacted, any information of that nature will remain confidential."

"Well what can you tell us?"

Warner ignored the question, and pointed to a woman in the front row with her hand up. "Yes?"

"What efforts are you making to find Gerard Williamson?" The reporter asked.

"Well for a start, we've got teams of detectives canvassing the area around the murder scene looking for witnesses or any information that might lead us to his current location. All our patrols have his photograph, and as you would have seen on the news last night, we've made a public appeal for anyone who's seen him to contact the police. His photo has been circulated to the press, and appeared in your paper this morning, on page three I believe."

"Have you found the car you suspect Gerard Williamson took from outside the prison yet?"

"Not yet, but we are confident we'll find it soon. No efforts are being spared in that regard."

"Do you think he's still in the Wellington area?"

"Again, that calls for speculation. Police in all regions are being kept fully informed."

"Do you think Gerard Williamson is a danger to the general public?" A TV3 reporter asked.

"I certainly feel that as long as he is at liberty, the public should be aware of the potential risk he presents, especially to children. Although he's yet to be convicted of a crime, the kidnapping and attempted murder charges he's facing, not to mention his escape from prison and assault on his lawyer, make him a potentially dangerous individual. Members of the public should not approach him. Anyone with information regarding his whereabouts should ring the police immediately. Now if you'll all excuse me, I have a job to do. The press will be advised of any new developments."

Warner walked away from the barrage of questions that followed him out of the room. As soon as he'd passed through the door, reporters scrambled to file their stories, ghouls on the run.

# CHAPTER 6 - WEDNESDAY MORNING

After a good night's sleep, Gerard felt a hundred percent better. Eager to reconnoitre the places he'd seen advertised in the paper the previous day, he dressed quickly.

While browsing the 'to lease' section, Gerard had discovered that small units weren't very common. Most places could be discounted straight away because they were either too large, or in a location that wouldn't allow him the privacy he required.

The seven potentials he'd found were spread all around the district. Two were out in Porirua, twenty-eight kilometres north of Wellington, the others in various parts of the Hutt Valley.

Gerard took a map from a drawer in the kitchen and unfolded it on the table. He made himself a coffee and some toast, and then sat back down to plan his route. After marking the location of each potential site on the map, it became obvious that starting with the two in Porirua, so he'd be driving against the rush-hour traffic heading into Wellington from further up the coast, made the most sense. That way he should have a clear run over the Hayward's Hill to the one in Upper Hutt, before heading back down the valley to the three in Lower Hutt. The last possibility was in Petone only thirty minutes from home.

The route was roughly triangular and covered approximately 70 kilometres. He figured it would take him just over two hours to do the circuit by the time he'd had a brief look at the outside of each property. To reduce the risk of being identified, he wouldn't contact any real estate agents until he'd found a premise that looked promising.

By the time Gerard finished his breakfast it was 7 a.m. He tucked the map and list into his jacket pocket, went down to the garage, and pulled the bike out of his locker.

As Gerard turned out of the garage and rode down the hill towards town, a stunning morning greeted him. Once past the old monastery on his right, a spectacular view of the city spread out before him.

Once again the harbour was calm. Even the wind-turbine,

situated high up on the Brooklyn Hill, stood motionless on the skyline.

Gerard could see two red tugs guiding a container ship to the wharf far below him, all three craft reflected in the waters stillness. Off to the right, a hazy Hutt Valley disappeared into the distance. A few kilometres to his left, the telecommunications mast on top of Mount Kaukau, Wellington's highest point, towered into the sky above bush-clad hills.

Judging by the amount of activity out on the water, Gerard guessed a fair few people had phoned in sick this morning, not that he could blame them. He counted eight yachts, four power boats, two jet skis, and eight kayakers, and it was still early. Two yachts had their large number one jibs up, hanging limply as their skippers looked for the hint of breeze. The other yachts, with sails unfurled, hadn't bothered trying to sail on such a still morning. Instead they were motoring out towards the harbour entrance and Cook Straight in hopes of finding a breeze.

On a day like today Gerard wished it was legal to ride without a helmet, to feel the warm breeze rush through his hair. Still, he was doing better than the poor sods stuck in prison, the roof of which he could just make out on the hilltop across Evans Bay less than a kilometre away.

**********

"Hey boss, did you see this morning's *DomPost*? The Williamson murder made the front page."

Warner looked up from a pile of paperwork on his desk and saw Blondie holding a steaming cup of coffee in each hand. "Yeah, I saw that. It was on the news last night too, both the six and ten o'clock. The media's whipped everyone into a frenzy. The switchboard's running hot with possible sightings."

"So what now? Gerard must know he left prints all over the scene. That can't be a good sign."

Warner took a sip of the coffee Blondie had placed before him then nodded. "I know. He's got nothing to lose, and that scares me."

Blondie looked at the stack of folders piled high on Warner's desk. "So what's with the old files?"

"I've pulled all the unsolved cases that relate to violence on children over the last ten or so years. Something in one of them might indicate Gerard's involvement and give us a lead. After reading his psych evaluation, I can't believe Bourne was an isolated incident."

"You really think he's hurt kids before?"

"I'd almost bet my pension on it." Warner said, putting the cup down and looking up at Blondie. "So, I'm going to stay here and coordinate the teams checking out possible sightings of Williamson and finish going through these files. While I do that, I want you try to find Gerard's mother. We can inform her of Nathan's death, but more importantly, she might have information that will help us locate Gerard. You know the drill. Sheryl said Gympie didn't she?"

**********

Gerard called the real estate agent for the Petone property from a phone booth when he got back to town. It was just after ten.

"Hi, my name's Tom Renfrew, I've rung about the workshop you have for lease in Petone ... the one in Cornish Street. Is it still available?"

"Why yes it is."

Gerard listened to the agent do his spiel about the property for a minute before the agent asked him when it would be convenient for him to view the property.

"Today if that's possible." Gerard said. "Yes I know where it is. In an hour? Sure that's great. Yes I have plenty of time to get there. Okay, I'll see you then."

Gerard liked the unit he'd seen in Petone the best. It had a good feel to it. Located on a small side street just off the main drag, the street's residents were predominantly owner operated businesses—an auto electrician, rug importer, muffler shop, a ceramic tile showroom, and a few others. Gerard was reasonably sure they wouldn't be hanging around much in the evenings or weekends.

The rug importer next door would be his closest neighbour. Gerard had already checked out their opening hours from a sign in the front window. They were 9:00 a.m. until 5:30 p.m. Monday to Friday.

*Perfect.*

The building itself was divided into two units. The walls were tilt-slab concrete which Gerard figured would be reasonably soundproof.

Painted plain white on the outside, apart from its large steel roller door, the unit was nondescript and unassuming, built for practicality not for show. Entry to the unit was gained through a heavy wooden door to the right of the main roller door. To the right of that was a tall narrow window protected by a steel security grill.

A faded sign that said 'Sutcliffe Mower Services' hung above the wooden door. Either Mr Sutcliffe had done well for himself, and had moved to a more salubrious neighbourhood, or he was back mowing lawns for one of the franchises again.

At the end of the street, a gravelled walkway meandered up the gully through the bush. The path followed a small stream and eventually led to an old reservoir once used to supply drinking water to the area. The banks of the stream were resplendent in native ferns, lichens and mosses. Mature trees teemed with birdlife.

Gerard remembered walking up to the reservoir once as a twelve year old with his parents for a picnic. Gerard found it hard to believe a place so beautiful could be such a short distance from the concrete ugliness of the factories and warehouses less than a kilometre away.

# CHAPTER 7 - WEDNESDAY AFTERNOON

Andy Thompson and Chris Spacey sat down for lunch after a busy morning. To their relief, there were no surprise parcels today.

"At least I slept last night," Chris said as he sat poking at his food. "I was afraid I'd dream of bloody fingers again. Luckily I conked right out."

"I know what you mean," Andy said. "I've had the odd nightmare myself."

Christ tried to forget about bloody fingers and focus on other aspects of his work. "So what are we going to do about that new drug ... Jesus Christ!" Chris sat stunned as Andy poured a quarter of a bottle of hot-sauce over his lunch. "I bet you'd eat cardboard if it had chilli on it."

Andy ignored Chris's comments, changing the subject back to the dealer. "I've been thinking. Let's meet at the station later tonight, grab a car, park outside the club, and try to spot the guy as he leaves. If we do, we'll stop him on the street and see if he's carrying."

"He may have sold out by then is the only problem."

"But if he's clever, the only time he'll have drugs in his possession is to and from the club."

"Sounds like a plan. How does 1:00 a.m. sound? That should give us enough time to be in position before the club closes."

"1:00 a.m. it is then." Andy said before picking up a shaker and proceeding to cover the top of the chilli sauce with pepper.

Chris couldn't believe what he was seeing. "Jesus mate. Have you got a death wish?"

**********

When Ashna Patel finished eating her lunch in the courtyard of Redford School, she went looking for her friend James. Ashna was the youngest of three children. Her family had lived in the Wellington suburb of Mount Victoria for twenty-two years after emigrating from the Gujarat province of India.

Ashna's parents owned a profitable food importing business. Her two older brothers, aged 13 and 15, worked in the family business after school, learning the ropes for when they would eventually take over the running of the business. They were the new Kiwis living the Kiwi dream. The dream thus far had been a pleasant one.

Ashna and her family lived in a comfortable four-bedroom house in Austin Street. The house didn't have a harbour view, so it had been cheaper than others nearby, but the lower price had enabled them to clear their mortgage a few years ago.

When Mr. and Mrs. Patel had first purchased the property, the area was predominantly multiple occupancy flats. As more and more owner-occupiers moved in, replacing the renters, the area had become more desirable. Over the past ten years, the neighbourhood had been improving steadily. House prices in Mount Victoria were now some of the highest in Wellington. Being a short walk to town made it very convenient, and people were willing to pay extra to live close to the action.

They'd thought about selling up and buying a bigger place further out in the suburbs a couple of times, but never did. The Patel family liked being at the centre of things, being able to walk to school or work as well as the library, theatres, and cafés.

Ashna was another consideration. She loved going to Redford School and was an excellent student. Her parents were reluctant to make her change to a new school when she was doing so well. They could have sent her to one of the state schools, but Redford School had a great reputation and it was only a short walk from home. The extra cost of tuition didn't matter to them. They worked hard so their kids could have opportunities.

**********

Gerard parked up outside the Petone workshop, lit a cigarette, and waited. He was a few minutes early. The agent arrived dead on time and greeted him outside the front door, key in hand, ready to open up the building for inspection.

"Hi you must be Mr. Renfrew. I'm Stephen." The agent shook Gerard's hand.

"Pleased to meet you Stephen."

"Well, let's start shall we?" Stephen said over his shoulder as he turned the key and stepped into the building. "The front of the building, as you can see, is the office area."

The entry had a narrow reception lobby with a Formica counter dividing it from an area that would normally contain a desk, filing cabinet and shelving.

"The office is on the small side, but it's clean and bright. You can get into the workshop through this internal door here." The agent opened a door to his left. "And, as you can see, the workshop is quite spacious."

Stephen led Gerard into what was approximately 1000 square feet of workshop. A solid wooden packing bench ran down one side of the open space, and there was a hoist running on a rail suspended from the ceiling.

"This electric hoist will lift 2 tons. Great for getting heavy stuff on and off the back of delivery trucks, and the roller door's got a remote. The amenities are at the back. There's a toilet and small kitchen, just through that end door. The room used to be a lock up for dangerous goods, but the owners converted it into staff facilities 15 years or so ago. The toilet is just through that door there," the agent said, pointing at a door leading off to the right of the staff room. "It's got a hand basin and separate toilet cubicle."

Gerard walked into the staff room and peeked inside the bathroom. Everything he needed was right here. He could live here for months if he had to.

"Is there much activity around this area in the evening? I'm a sculptor and quite often work at night. I don't want a lot of noise distracting me."

Gerard lied about being a sculptor, but the part about not wanting distractions was certainly true.

"The businesses around here are pretty much nine-to-five. I wouldn't imagine there'd be much happening after six. You might get the odd walker or mountain biker using the track at the end of the street in the early evenings, but it's not the sort of place people hang around after dark."

The agent pointed upward. "Those big spotlights will give you plenty of light to work at night, and the skylights let in plenty of light in during the day. Not many external windows in the place, but if you're worried about security this place is very safe. The window in the front office even has a security grill."

"Yes I noticed," Gerard said nodding his head.

Gerard's mind buzzed with excitement. An automatic door meant he could drive straight into the workshop without ever having to get out of the van. The workshop was more than big enough for any preparation he'd need to do. There was plenty of soundproofing in the concrete walls, and it had kitchen and toilet facilities. Plus, it had the bonus of a lockable room with no windows! Gerard couldn't believe his luck.

*It's perfect.*

"What's the story on the lease?" Gerard asked.

"Well, as you can see, the place is empty," the agent said, sensing a commission. "You can move in as soon as a 12-month lease is signed, and the rent and bond are paid. Do you want to do that today by any chance?" Stephen said, attempting to close the deal before the guy had time to go cold and change his mind.

Gerard pretended to think a few moments. "Okay, you've convinced me." Soon he'd be hunting again, and feeling so good. "I brought the necessary deposit with me on the off chance the place was suitable. I'm keen to get back to work as soon as I can. It's been too long."

"Why don't we go to my office and get the paperwork sorted then? Do you know where my office is? If not, just follow me. It isn't far."

"I think I know the way, but I'll follow you just to be sure."

Before 30 minutes had passed, Gerard had signed the lease. It was a standard Law Society form. Gerard didn't even bother to read the fine print. He'd seen them before. Reaching into his pocket, he pulled out a wad of notes. Half was for the security bond, the remainder for the first month's rental. Stephen took the cash, smiled briefly, and counted it out before writing a receipt.

Formalities completed, the two men shook hands. Stephen handed Gerard the keys, and the remote for the roller door.

"Well Mr. Renfrew, for the next twelve months she's all yours."

It was only 2:40 p.m. The meeting with the real estate agent and the signing of the lease had taken less than an hour. The keys made a satisfying jingle in Gerard's pocket as he left the real estate office. Walking the short distance to the van, Gerard climbed in and decided to go shopping for some of the gear he'd need. He saw no point in wasting any time.

A hardware store would be his first stop, somewhere that had all the tools and building materials in the one place. He remembered one in Kaiwharawhara, just off the motorway on the way back towards the city. Gerard composed a mental list as he drove—bolt cutters, a slide bolt, a couple of padlocks, soundproofing batts, duct tape, some timber, a few hand tools, tool belt, and most important of all, a shiny new pair of secateurs.

A camping store was next for sleeping bags, camp stretchers, gas stove, nylon rope, and a hunting knife. Then he went to the supermarket for a broom, cleaning gear, bandages, disinfectant, sterile tape, enough food to last a week or so, and some bottled water. Gerard selected what goods he needed quickly and paid cash.

Gerard's hunting plans included a wooden crate, so after he finished shopping, he went for a drive around the Petone industrial area. It wasn't long before he found what he was looking for.

A large warehouse, down one of the side streets, had a stack of pallets and crates out front. He parked the van on the street and went into a door marked 'reception'. After speaking nicely to a woman behind the counter, she happily let Gerard take whatever he wanted.

"It's all off to the tip in any case," she said

Gerard picked a crate roughly a metre wide, a metre high, and just under a metre long, large enough to transport a child, but small enough to fit comfortably through the sliding door and into the back of the van. After manhandling the crate into the van alongside his other purchases, he drove back towards his new unit.

As he neared the unit, Gerard triggered the remote for the roller door and pulled straight into the building, closing the door behind him. He hummed a song from the radio as he unpacked. It was a snug little place, out of the way, and private. He could see himself being very happy here, very happy indeed.

After unloading his purchases, Gerard drove to his bank and set up an automatic payment for the rent. He also deposited some of the surplus cash he hadn't used when purchasing the van and the other gear so there would be enough money in the account for three months rent. That way he wouldn't need to remember when payments were due. Then he made a quick trip to the power company to transfer the power account into the name of Tom Renfrew. He paid the cash deposit, and filled in a direct debit form to have the monthly electricity charges deducted directly from his account as well. He wouldn't need a phone or rubbish collection. The only disposals he had planned, he'd do himself, secretly in the dead of night.

Once the banking and utilities were sorted, Gerard couldn't resist going for a drive around a couple of schools while there was still a little daylight left. He'd never dreamed he'd have such an ideal place so soon, and his eagerness to find a new hunting ground made him tremble with excitement.

When he reached a school in Newtown, Gerard slowed down. The school had closed hours ago and there were no cars behind him so he had no reason to hurry. After doing a circuit of the school he knew it wasn't suitable for his purposes. It was too exposed from a four story block of flats overlooking the only gate.

*Next*

It had been a long day, but Gerard wanted to check out one last school in Mount Victoria. It was on his way home anyway. After Gerard drove around the Basin Reserve, he turned right up Pirie Street. Turning right again into Brougham Street he drove another block where, on his left, he found the school he was looking for, Redford School.

After doing a circuit of the school, Gerard turned the van around, and drove around a second time in the opposite direction. He noticed a locked gate set into a six-foot high brick wall topped with spikes of wrought-iron on the schools southern end. Inside the wall was a small playing field. The narrow gate looked rarely used. The rust on its bars, chain, and old padlock were evidence of that. Gerard figured that in all likelihood, the gate was permanently locked.

If Gerard decided to use this gate to gain access to the school, the walls on either side of the gate would obscure any view of him or his van from inside the school grounds until he was ready to make his move. Then, by re-locking the gate on his way out, he would prevent anyone following him.

On the other side of the street, opposite the gate, there was a vacant section. It looked as though some new construction was due to start.

The section had been levelled, and a series of pegs driven into the ground, indicating where the new foundations would be placed. The houses on either side of the empty lot were typical 1920s single bay villas, well kept, with tiny gardens or car pads in the front, and long narrow gardens to the rear. Overall, it was a pretty nice and tidy middle-income neighbourhood.

*I'll check it out more thoroughly tomorrow morning.*

While driving around, a plan of attack had been forming in Gerard's mind. He knew of a hardware shop that sold peel-and-stick vinyl letters. He could put a company name on the side of the van, and then spend some time watching the neighbourhood and the school's routine while pretending to do preparation work for the construction project. With a tape measure and tool belt, and wearing a work shirt and hard hat, he'd look like any other tradesman. With a bit of builders gear in the back of the van to complete his disguise, he'd be totally unremarkable, and practically invisible. He just needed to think of a name.

"Chris Thompson Construction," Gerard said aloud, trying the name out for size.

That would do the trick, not to mention put the wind up those two cops if they ever found out he'd used it in their honour.

Gerard's mind was racing now. If he hurried, he had just enough time to buy the letters and a hardhat before the shop closed.

**********

For most of the afternoon Warner organised officers to check leads received from the public, and went through the files he'd pulled from the archives. As he quickly browsed each old case he looked for anything unusual, anything at all that might indicate Gerard's involvement. Then, just as he went to close a file relating to a murdered eight-year-old, a single line in a coroner's report caught his attention.

Warner stopped. He flipped back through the pages of the report, his eyes scanning quickly. An employee had discovered the body of a strangled child stuffed into a wheelie bin behind the fast food restaurant where he worked. Forensics hadn't had much to go on. There were no fibres or hair found on the child or the child's clothing, no witnesses, and no hint as to the identity of the murderer.

The police had poured huge resources into the investigation over a period of six months, public appeals were made, and rewards offered for information, all to no avail. The four-year-old file was still open, but listed as 'inactive', which was another way of saying the police had no idea who committed the crime. It didn't happen often, but in this case, and despite their best efforts and every resource available, the police had struck out.

The line that attracted Warner's attention mentioned that the tip of one of the victim's fingers was missing. The wound hadn't affected the bone. Just the fleshy part at the tip of the finger was severed. None the less, the injury would have hurt like hell with all the nerve endings located in that region.

No sexual molestation had take place, but there had been severe bruising on the lad's legs and back, indicating he'd taken quite a beating prior to his death. Police investigating the case were suspicious that the bruises were a result of excessive discipline dished out by one of the family, but nothing was ever proven, and both parents had willingly taken and passed polygraphs.

Forensics also found an adhesive residue on the victim's legs and arms indicating the boy had been trussed up at some stage. Upon testing, the residue turned out to be the adhesive component used in New Zealand's most popular brand of duct tape, a tape far too common to be of any help in the police hunt for the perpetrator.

The severing of the finger, and the culprit using duct tape to immobilise their victim wasn't much to go on, but it gave Warner some hope he'd found a link to Gerard.

The last clue police had in the old case were sightings of an unfamiliar white van parked at various places along the route the boy took to school on two consecutive days prior to his disappearance. Witnesses told police that the van had a company name on its side, but none could remember what the name was. Some witnesses thought the van belonged to a plumber, others a builder. Most agreed it looked like a tradesman's van as opposed to a delivery vehicle, but beyond that details were sketchy.

Police put out a plea to the public asking anyone who had been driving a white van in that area, on those particular days, to come forward so their vehicle could be eliminated from their enquiries.

Two van owners had come forward, but witnesses agreed neither was the van in question. To this day, the owner of the mystery van remains just that, a mystery.

Nonetheless, Warner's instincts were starting to twitch, instincts that had served him well over his years as an investigator.

"Is it just coincidence, the van, the finger, the tape? Or was that you Gerard?" Warner mumbled to himself.

Gerard had used a white van when he abducted Leonard Bourne as well. Maybe using a white van was part of Gerard's M.O., one of his little idiosyncrasies. If so, it was time to start looking for the proverbial needle in a haystack. It would be a long shot. White vans were everywhere. But what else did they have to go on?

Blondie knocked once then entered Warner's office. "Williamson's mum died last year of bowel cancer."

Warner closed the file in front of him and looked up. "That's a shame, but not to worry, I've got another idea."

Warner told Blondie about the inactive case he'd found, and how it might link to Gerard. "If this was Gerard's handiwork, and I think there's a chance it was, then his search for another white van could be the key. People are creatures of habit, especially crazy ones. Maybe using a white van is one of his"

"But there are thousands ..."

"I know. But how many have been sold in the last forty-eight hours? He's going to need transportation sometime. Gerard's way too smart to drive a stolen car for long."

"Sounds logical but ..."

Warner could hear a touch of panic creeping into Blondie's voice. "Look focus on Toyotas. Check the dealers in town and the Hutt Valley first. We know he has plenty of cash. Don't worry about private sales yet. I doubt he'll waste time trying to buy privately. Give everyone you talk to a photo of Gerard so they can phone us if he turns up later on."

"Am I meant to do this all on my own?"

"Drag in a couple of helpers if you can. Look, I realise it's going to take time, but there's nothing else to go on at the moment."

"Okay Boss, I'd better get moving. The yards will be closing soon."

"I know it's a needle in a haystack. Do what you can today and then start again in the morning. In the meantime I'm going to finish reading the last of these files. Maybe something else will show up."

'A needle in a haystack' seemed an understatement to Blondie. To her it felt more like a needle in a field of haystacks.

When Blondie got to her desk, she phoned the Area Commander and asked for some extra manpower. He told her he'd do his best. Encouraged, she picked up the phone and started ringing.

"Hello, my name is Detective Green from the Wellington

Police. I'm sorry to bother you, but we urgently need a list of all the white vans you've sold in the last 48 hours, especially Toyotas."

The Area Commander rang back fifteen minutes later and told Blondie she'd have two constables joining her first thing in the morning. He wanted this case solved before the heat started coming down from above. Nobody likes it when a sadistic nut case is running around, especially one who likes to chop off children's fingers. It wasn't a good look for the city or the police.

**********

By 6:15 p.m. Gerard was back in Petone with the self-adhesive letters for the van. He made a mental list of the jobs he wanted to do in preparation for tomorrow. First, he took five minutes and stored away his earlier purchases. The food, water, and first aid supplies went into the kitchen cupboards. Surplus tools and hardware went into a couple of large drawers suspended beneath the workbench.

With his supplies sorted, putting a slide bolt on the kitchen door was next on the list. The old staff room would make an excellent cell once he could secure it from the outside.

After turning on the spotlights, Gerard got to work. Half an hour later he slid the bolt neatly into place.

"More secure than the remand wing I reckon," Gerard said, chuckling to himself.

Next he picked up the bag containing the stick-on letters. Putting them on the van would require patience, especially if he wanted the job to look professional.

Gerard started by making a straight and level line on the van's side with a pencil. Then he took his time to work out the correct spacing for the letters. Once the layout was marked out, the actual placement of the letters didn't take long. After an hour or so of concentrated effort, Gerard wiped the letters one last time with a damp cloth to remove any remaining air bubbles, and stepped back to admire his handiwork.

"Chris Thompson Construction," Gerard said, loving the

sound of it. "Looking good Mr Thompson!"

Gerard loaded a few empty boxes and some of the builder's gear into the back of the van ready for the morning, locked up the workshop, and then drove back to the apartment in Roseneath.

After having a long hot shower, Gerard realised he'd been so busy he'd forgotten to have lunch. It was no wonder his stomach was rumbling like a tumble dryer full of tennis shoes. Quickly changing into his Tom Renfrew outfit he strolled down into town.

Parking would have been easy to find at this hour, but Gerard didn't want his van out in the open with the new name on it, not yet anyway. He didn't want to run any risk of someone stealing or damaging it. Too many street kids hung around town these days, some of which seemed to have an uncontrollable urge to tag anything that wasn't moving. He could have taken the bike, but he might want to have a few beers. Failing a breathalyser at some checkpoint on the way home was the last thing he needed.

*It's only a 30-minute walk, why risk it?*

After an uneventful walk into town, and a late dinner of chilli con queso and a couple of burritos with extra jalapeños at a Mexican restaurant in Cuba Street, Gerard popped into an alleyway around the back of the restaurant and made his way to where they put their rubbish. Opening a wheelie bin, he rummaged around for a few moments before coming up with two glass jars, slightly wider at the base than the top, each with its distinctive yellow top. These he wiped with a piece of paper before putting them into his jacket pocket.

*These should come in handy real soon.*

**********

It was nearly 9:30 p.m. James Warner's bedtime. His parents were strict about him being in bed on time. A twelve-year-old needed his sleep.

As James put on his pyjamas, he thought about his best friend at school, Ashna Patel. He liked the way she made him laugh.

Plus she shared his interested in mice, frogs, and insects. She sat next to him in class, and even though she was a girl, James thought she was pretty cool.

Ashna and James had been best friends since his father's promotion to Detective Inspector and the Warner family transferred to Wellington two years ago. James was glad they'd moved. He hadn't had a friend like Ashna in Palmerston North.

*I'm going to marry Ashna when I get older. One day, I might even kiss her!*

James got a ride to school each morning. Both Robert and Julia felt a twenty-minute walk to Redford School was too far to be safely negotiated by someone his age. James always protested, saying he was twelve now, and other kids walked or caught the bus to school by themselves, but despite James's objections, Robert and Julia were having none of it.

Since Gerard's escape Robert Warner would have put James in a taxi before he'd let him walk to school on his own. He'd seen Leonard Bourne cowering in the back bedroom when they'd busted into the apartment to arrest Gerard. He'd seen the terror in his eyes, seen his tears, and seen his fingerless hand wrapped in a bloody rag.

*********

After putting the chilli jars into his pocket, Gerard made the decision to wander down to a club he knew on Courtenay Place to see if he could score some speed. It was on his way home anyway. He just hoped the dealer he knew was still hanging out there.

He liked how speed made him feel. After a couple of snorts he'd see things more clearly, his surroundings would come alive, and he'd noticed little things he normally missed. It also heightened his pleasure when he caused pain, making his every nerve tingle with excitement.

The streets were busy with people. The early movies had just come out, while others like Gerard, had finished eating a meal at one of the many restaurants in the area and were on their way home. Others were having a night out on the town, just drifting from bar to bar checking out the scene.

In an attempt to be as inconspicuous as possible, Gerard tagged along behind a group of six who'd just come out of a Thai restaurant, and were walking in the same direction. He followed them for five minutes or so before turning right into Courtenay Place and merging with a group of blokes of similar age.

As Gerard neared The Cloud Nine Club, he passed a raucous group of young women dressed in devil costumes heading in the opposite direction. One of the women had a sign hung around her neck saying 'Soon To Be Married'. The group were in good spirits, laughing and whistling at the guys they passed, obviously drunk, but having a great time. No doubt, they'd have the hangovers from hell, to match their outfits, in the morning.

As he neared the club, Gerard could hear music drifting out to the street. Many of the tables set up on the footpath behind a low fence constructed of potted plants and lattice were occupied with patrons having a late snack or drink. The bouncer, a large Polynesian man wearing a spotless black suit and sporting a huge smile as white as his shirt, nodded and opened the door for him.

Once Gerard's eyes adjusted to the darkness, he saw a U-shaped bar that swept around in a graceful curve protruding into the room. Eight or so tables were on the street side of the bar, a slightly quieter area preferred by couples who sat deep in conversation with heads close together. A row of padded stools lined the bar. Beyond that, some taller tables, some with stools, surrounded the dance floor. Gerard didn't recognise the music, but it had the punters on their feet.

Gerard walked past the front tables, pulled out a stool near the middle of the bar, and sat down. From this position he could see both sides of the club without having to crane his neck around. He ordered a Corona, tipping the young barman when it arrived.

Thirty or so people were dancing. The sign out front had said it was ladies night, and the half price bubbly certainly had some of them going. There were a few couples dancing, but the majority were groups of females. More than one of the women looked as though she'd had a glass of champagne too many.

"I don't want champagne I want real-pagne," a young woman giggled to the barman, as she wobbled on overly high heels to Gerard's left.

Gerard heard her play on words.

*Give me some time girly. I'll give you some real pain.*

One group of women in their forties danced like maniacal go-go girls, hair flailing, arms pumping, shaking every part of their bodies to the music. It was quite a sight. Gerard smiled as he watched them. He admired people who could let loose, even if they were fuelled by alcohol. He'd always been more reserved in public, more aloof. Only when he was somewhere private and in control did he really come out of his shell.

Gerard's eyes casually scanned the crowd, looking for his supplier. Just as he finished his first beer, Gerard notice him come out of the men's toilets and walk to a back table where he sat down next to an attractive woman with short dark hair, and an even shorter black skirt.

Gerard leaned towards the barman and said in a low voice, "I'm assuming you know the guy with the pony tail." The barman nodded without saying a word.

"After you get me another beer would you mind attracting his attention, let him know I'd like a word?" Gerald slid a note across the bar.

After placing Gerard's beer on a coaster in front of him, the barman made a subtle gesture towards the other side of the room and then nodded towards Gerard.

Gerard quietly sipped his beer, and waited.

A few minutes later the guy with the ponytail was standing next to him, ordering a round of drinks. He turned his head towards Gerard. "You looking for me?"

"Yeah," Gerard said softly. "If you've still got some speed I'd be interested."

"Not a problem my friend. Go into the gents. I'll join you in a tick."

Gerard left his half-finished beer on the bar and strolled

casually toward the men's toilets at the rear of the club. Double swing doors led to a tiled bathroom with three urinals and two stalls. There was no one else in the room, so Gerard leaned against the sink bench and waited.

"Okay let's sort you out eh?" The dealer said a few minutes later, opening a small tin, and revealing a number of clear envelopes containing a white powder. "How much do you want?"

Gerard passed over a handful of notes and received four envelopes. "Thanks," Gerard said, before putting all but one of the envelopes in his pocket. "This will certainly make the walk back up the hill a lot more pleasant."

"No problem. Come and see me again if you want more. I'm always here till closing."

"I will. Thanks."

Gerard entered one of the cubicles and closed the door. Using the top of the cistern as a table and one of the lawyer's credit cards he made two lines of white powder. Then, he rolled up twenty-dollar note and snorted a line of speed up each nostril before going back to the bar to finish his beer.

The dancers were still at it, now they were doing the twist. He couldn't help but chuckle under his breath. The speed had given him a nice little high. He felt better than he had in days.

When Gerard walked out of the bar and headed towards home a few minutes later, he was buzzing with excitement. Tomorrow was only one sleep away.

*Let the hunt begin.*

# CHAPTER 8 - THURSDAY MORNING

At 1:00 a.m. Chris and Andy met at the station. They signed out an unmarked car and drove straight to Courtenay Place where they parked across the road from The Cloud Nine Club.

The spot they'd chosen was in the shadows, yet still gave the two detectives a reasonable view of the club's front door. They slumped down in their seats to wait for the club to close.

It wasn't long before the number of patrons exiting the club increased notably. Andy and Chris focused their attention on each male that walked out.

When a well-dressed guy with a ponytail appeared Chris sat up slightly and peered intently across the street. "Hey Andy, that looks like our guy."

"Sure does. Nice looking lady on his arm too. Man look at those legs."

Chris ignored Andy's comment, and concentrated on the suspected dealer. "Let's wait until he gets to his car. I'll bet you ten bucks that's his red BMW." Chris said pointing up the road. "See the new one with the mags near the corner. Once he pulls out his keys we'll pay him a friendly visit."

"Sneak attack from the rear, I'll frisk the girl."

"Believe me mate. She's not hiding anything under that dress."

Chris started their car. "Remember, we go in fast so he doesn't have time to toss anything. I'll go around the front of the BMW, you take rear guard okay?"

"Okay big guy, let's rock n' roll."

Just as the couple reached the car, the unmarked police car screeched to a halt beside them. Chris and Andy had their doors open ready to move before they'd even come to a stop. As soon as Chris yanked on the hand brake they came out sprinting.

"Police! Get your hands in the air. In the air I said. Now!"

Chris wasted no time getting around the front of the car and stood menacingly in front of the guy who, although reasonably tall, looked small by comparison. Chris could see the guy's mind ticking over as he calculated his odds of escape. Chris crouched, ready to pounce if necessary.

Just as the guy started to turn, tempted to sprint for it, Andy's voice rang out from behind him. "Let me guess, you're an optimist. You always think of your brain as being half full. Right?"

The guy hesitated.

Andy took a step towards him. "Now don't make me set my trained gorilla on you. Believe me pal, you don't want that."

Seeing the hopelessness of his situation, the guy with the pony tail put his hands up. The girl also put her hands up. As she did, her skirt rode up, making the short skirt even shorter.

Andy moved behind the guy. "Okay, now spread your feet apart and put your hands on the top of the car." Andy said.

Chris relaxed. "You're okay Miss, just stay where you are. It's your boyfriend we want a word with."

"What's going on?" The man said complying with Andy's order. "We haven't done anything. Why are you stopping us?"

"We've had information that leads us to believe you've been selling drugs. So let's just see what you've got in your pockets shall we?" Andy kicked the guys feet a little further apart, and pushed him against the car. "If you're clean then you and your girlfriend can be on your way. If not, well that's another story."

Before Andy put his hand into the man's pockets, he leaned forward, his hand in the middle of the dealers back, and whispered into his ear. "Now I'm not going to get a surprise and stick myself with a needle doing this, am I? Cause if I do ..."

"No," the guy said, looking none too happy.

Reaching his hand into the man's right-hand jacket pocket, Andy pulled out a large wad of bank notes.

"Did you win lotto or have you been a bad boy?" Andy said.

The left pocket contained a tin that had once contained a popular brand of cough lozenges. Opening the tin revealed a dozen small transparent packets containing a white substance.

"What have we here? Wouldn't be drugs by any chance, would it pal? Read him his rights partner," Andy said, taking the handcuffs from his belt and putting them on the man's wrists.

Chris pulled out his notebook. "Alright, what's your name and address?" After jotting down the man's details, Chris pulled out a printed card and read what was on it.

"You are under arrest for possession with the intent to distribute a class-A drug. You have the right to a lawyer ..."

When Chris had finished, the dealer nodded in his girlfriend's direction. "Is it okay if she takes my car home? I don't want it left here. It'll get towed in the morning if it's not moved. Besides, she's got no way of getting home."

"Sorry, but this cars going to the impound yard to be thoroughly searched. Now Miss, I'll need your full name and address." Chris had his pencil poised over his pad again.

After getting the young woman's details, Chris suggested she catch a cab home.

"I'd prefer to stay where I am at the moment."

"Suit yourself," Chris said with a shrug before putting the dealer into the back of the police car.

The girl stood a few yards away and watched. A few late-night revellers joined her, asking what was going on, who was being arrested, and why.

In police car, Chris and Andy started their normal line of questioning, testing the dealer out to see if he might cough up a bigger fish in exchange for some leniency.

Andy had just started his favourite line about how possession with intent to supply a class-A narcotic carried a maximum sentence of up to life imprisonment, when the dealer noticed the picture of Williamson clipped to the dashboard.

"Hey I know that guy."

A tingle of excitement coursed through Chris's body. He took the photo and held it closer to the man's face "You've seen this guy? Are you sure?"

"Yeah, I'm sure," the dealer said, peering closer at the photo. "He looks a little different than in this shot, but I've definitely seen the guy. I've got a good memory for faces."

"You mean recently?" Chris asked.

"It was recent alright."

"Where was this?" Chris said, grabbing his pad again.

"Can you cut me a little slack if I help you guys out?" the dealer enquired hopefully. "I can't do jail time."

"Help us catch this guy, and we'll do what we can." Chris told him.

"You're not just spinning me a line are you?" The dealer was suspicious, but he wanted to make a deal if at all possible. Jail was not his idea of a good place to spend a day let alone years. He'd heard rumours about what happened to good looking young men in jail.

"Look mate, you're in a deep trouble," Chris said, staring at the man in the back seat. "I suggest you take my word for it. Believe me. We want this guy a shitload more than we want the likes of you. Do you realise this is the guy who chopped off that Bourne kid's fingers, and most likely murdered his father? It's been all over the news. You'll be doing a public service helping us find the bastard."

"Yeah, we want him a lot more than you pal," agreed Andy.

The dealer looked at the picture once more. "I remember hearing something about that. So that's the guy eh?"

"That's him alright," Chris confirmed "A complete and utter bastard."

"Okay," the dealer said hesitantly. "It's not like I've got a lot of choice here."

"No you don't," Chris and Andy said in unison.

The dealer thought for a moment. "Right . . . well um . . . this guy came into the club."

"When was this?" Chris asked.

"Tonight around ten or so … definitely before eleven anyway. I got a nod that he wanted to see me, so I came over for a chat. He was looking to score some more speed. As you already know, I happened to have some available, so I met him in the gents and we did the business.

"So you've seen him before tonight." Andy said.

"He was here two or three weeks ago, mentioned the name of a friend of mine and wanted to score. He looked like he'd been hammering it a bit. Before that I'd never set eyes on him."

"So what did he say? Anything that might help us locate

him?" Chris asked.

The dealer put his hand to his forehead and tried to remember. "Um ... the only things he said were thanks, and that a quick line would make the walk back up the hill more enjoyable, or something like that. I didn't really talk to him."

"So he's local?" Andy asked.

"Sounded like it. He could have been spinning me a line, but he seemed genuine enough. It was just an offhand comment really."

"What would be the point of him trying to mislead you? Nothing really in it for him," Andy half questioned, half speculated.

"Anyway, he paid me then disappeared into a cubicle, probably to do a line or two. I went back to my table. He came out of the toilet a few minutes later, went to the bar, finished his beer and left."

"You said he looks different from the photograph," Andy said, pointing at the picture. "Different in what way?"

"He was wearing dark framed glasses, and his hair's darker and a bit shorter." The dealer nodded towards the picture. "But it was him alright."

Chris and Andy got out of the car for a quick confab, leaving the dealer locked in the back seat. The girl was still ten metres away, watching intently. She was alone again now. Rent-a-crowd had gotten bored with the lack of action, and had moved on in search of something more exciting.

Chris looked over Andy's shoulder, through the car window at the dealer as he spoke. "Do you think this guy's for real, or just trying to bullshit his way out of trouble?"

"I don't think he's lying," Andy said. "His body language makes me think he's telling the truth, or at least most of the truth. Wouldn't it be amazing if we could find Gerard again?"

"You wouldn't find me complaining."

"So, what do we do, let him go and hope like hell he phones us if Gerard comes back to the club? That could be a bit risky."

Chris scratched his head a moment. "If we keep Pretty Boy's drug tin with his prints on it for insurance, I reckon he'll do what we say. Plus we can get him to update Gerard's picture down at the station. We'll have a lot more chance of finding the bastard if people know what he looks like."

Andy nodded. "Then once Gerard is back behind bars, we'll have a little talk to our friend here about giving up his supplier and retiring from the drug business once and for all. Not that he needs to know that now of course."

"Sounds like a plan."

"Anyway," Andy said. "Why would he risk leaving town when he knows he'll end up with a warrant chasing him? All he has to do to make this whole mess go away is help us apprehend some psycho. I know what I'd do if I were him."

"Okay, well let's run the idea past him and see if he'll deal," Chris said. "He's too soft for prison, and I think he knows it."

Returning to the car, the two detectives laid out their terms. The dealer was more than happy to go along any plan that kept him out of jail.

"You take your girlfriend home. We'll be on your doorstep at seven sharp, and believe me you don't want to make us wait," Andy told him. "Oh and wear something that doesn't make you look like a fucking drug dealer okay?"

"Don't worry. I'll be out on the street waiting when you arrive."

Chris groaned as he looked at his watch. "Okay, well let's go get a few hours sleep. Get out of here. We'll see you in four and a half hours."

**********

Both Warner and Blondie arrived at the office before seven o'clock. Time was one luxury they didn't have, not if they were going to catch Williamson before he did something horrible.

The officers canvassing Williamson's office building had come up empty handed. Nor had the remainder of the old case files turned up anything relevant. If Williamson had been involved in any other crimes, he'd hid his involvement well.

The forensics report on Nathan Williamson's murder lay on

the desk in front of Warner. Gerard prints had been found on the car, the tape, and Nathan's watchstrap. This information, combined with Gerard's prints being found on the jar and the courier-pack sent to Chris and Andy proved beyond a shadow of a doubt Gerard had killed his father. Police had more than enough evidence to convict Gerard of the murder once they managed to arrest him. What they didn't have was any idea as to his current whereabouts, or how to find him apart from the 'white van' theory, and that was still a very big maybe.

Warner set the report aside. "How're you going with the car yards Blondie?"

"I've found sixteen vans sold in the last forty eight hours so far, none to a Williamson. Four were sold to women, so that leaves twelve to check out. But I've only scratched the surface. There's likely to be ten times that number by the time we finish ringing around today. Looks like we'll need to speak to all the salespeople involved, show them Gerard's picture, and see if any of them recognize him."

"Any suggestions on our next move?"

"How about to Canada, I hear the crime rate there's really low."

"If only." Warner smiled. "Okay, stick at it, but give me what you've got so far. As soon as the dealerships open I'll get to work checking them out. You can give me more as you find them."

"Okay, give me a minute. I'll go and print out a list for you."

Shortly after Blondie left the office, Warner's phone rang. He reached for the handset. "Warner."

"Hi, it's Chris Spacey, I'm glad you're in early." We've picked up some info on Gerard Williamson."

"Great. What have you got?"

"We've turned up a witness who's seen him in the last twelve hours or so. Seems your boy has altered his appearance. Thought we'd get the witness to work with one of the computer sketch people and get his picture updated. Plus we think we know roughly the area Gerard's holed up."

"Where are you now?"

"We're heading towards the station ... should be there in

fifteen or so.

"Well done. Once you get the witness in with a technician, come up and see me."

The phone call from Chris had buoyed Warner's spirits. He rang Blondie.

When she heard the news, she prayed the lead would turn into something concrete.

"They should be in my office in fifteen minutes or so," Warner said. "You should sit in on this."

Blondie looked forward to another meeting with the two detectives. It would be a nice break from thumbing through the yellow pages and trolling the automotive websites. She tucked an updated list for Warner into her pocket and strolled towards the bathroom. She had just enough time to touch up her makeup, run a brush through her hair, and make coffee.

*********

"Okay, you know the story here. We won't mention your drug dealing providing you do everything you can to help. Fuck us around, and you'll be locked up faster than a rabbit can fuck."

The dealer could hear the malice in Chris's voice. "Don't worry about me, I know what to do."

"When we get to the station, we'll put you in with a sketch artist and get you to update that picture of Williamson. That shouldn't take long. We've got one in the system already so you'll just need to get the glasses and hair right. Okay?"

"Okay."

"Once you've done that, the Detective Inspector in charge of the case, will interview you. Now remember, you were drinking in the club, we were showing Gerard's picture around, and you recognised him. You'd had a casual conversation with Williamson at the bar earlier in the evening. Now for fuck sake, keep it simple! Trying to be creative will only complicate things. Stick as close to the truth as you can, and only answer the questions the D.I. asks you. Once you're finished, ring me on my cell and tell me everything you've told him. Got it?"

"Yeah, I got it."

**********

Without knocking, Blondie entered Warner's office, placed the updated list and a coffee cup in front of him, and then plopped down on the chair opposite him to wait for the others.

Warner looked over the list and began planning a route that would enable him and his team to visit the car yards in the least amount of time. It would most likely take until lunchtime to get through the ones Blondie had identified so far, let alone those she'd come up with today. Warner could tell it was going to be another long day.

A few moments later there was a knock at the door.

"Enter," Warner said.

Chris smiled at Warner and then beamed at Blondie. Warner remained seated so Blondie followed his lead.

"Hey thanks for coming in guys," Warner said. "So, what have you got?"

"It's not a great deal, but it might narrow things down a bit," Chris replied. Chris knew how difficult it could be telling only part of the truth. But this way, with the dealer on lookout, if Gerard went back to the club they'd have the inside track to picking him up. In the meantime Chris wanted to protect the dealer as a future source of information. Every informer in their pocket was gold. The more informants they had, the more arrests they made. Information could often be the difference between success and failure in their game. Chris chose his words carefully.

"Well, we were making some enquiries to do with a drug case we've been working on in The Cloud Nine Club on Courtenay Place. We were also flashing Williamson's photo about, just on the off chance someone had seen him. Anyway, one of the patrons recognised Gerard, said he'd seen him earlier that evening."

"I had a feeling he was still in town," Blondie said.

"Anyway, this guy had a brief conversation with Williamson

at the bar, and said he'd mentioned walking home up the hill."

"Up the hill? So he might be staying in Mount Victoria or somewhere nearby." Warner said.

"That's what we figured," Chris said. "We've got the witness downstairs now doing a new composite. It seems Gerard's changed his appearance somewhat. He's got shorter hair and dark-framed glasses now. We should have the updated picture shortly."

"They'll bring the witness up here to you afterwards," Andy added.

"Well done guys, that's a start. Hey, I don't suppose you feel like showing this new picture to a few car yards on Kent Terrace in any spare time you've got?" Warner asked. "Apart from what you've just given us, all we've got to go on is a theory that Williamson might buy a white van. We think it's a little quirk of his."

"I'm compiling a list of the car yards that have sold vans in the last 48 hours." Blondie said. "Now we need to show them Williamson's picture and hope like hell someone recognizes him."

"I'm going to start doing the rounds as soon as they open this morning." Warner said. "It's going to be a hell of a long list by the time Blondie gets finished, any help you could give us would certainly be appreciated. I doubt we'll finish today. It may take a few days depending on how many turn up, and how far up the coast we go."

Andy looked at Chris who shrugged his shoulders. Andy wasn't that keen on doing the donkeywork for someone else's investigation, but he felt a part of the case. "I don't mind ... Chris?"

Chris was keen because it would give him a chance to see Blondie again, but he didn't want to seem too eager. "I suppose we could do a few for you."

"Great." Blondie said jumping to her feet. "Come to my office and I'll give you a copy of the list."

"Hey Andy, do you mind seeing if the witness is finished downstairs, maybe grab some copies of the new picture while I grab the list?"

"No problem, I'll see you back at the car in a few minutes."

Blondie led Chris down the hall while Andy disappeared downstairs.

"So, not many leads on this one so far?" Chris asked as they walked down the hallway to her office.

"No. You guys seem to be doing better than we are. Hey, thanks again for your help. We sure need it." Blondie turned her head and looking up into Chris's eyes.

*I wonder if he has a girlfriend.*

"I was hoping we might have a chance to help. Since we helped catch him the first time we kind of feel a part of it you know. Besides, we owe it to that nut-bar for sending us those bloody fingers."

"Yeah, Gerard's a strange one alright."

"I suppose you'll be working long hours until you find him again."

Chris wondered if it was too soon to ask her out. He'd hadn't seen a ring on her finger, not that that meant much these days

"Yeah, Warners got the whip out on this one. Hey maybe we could meet for a drink a bit later. You can tell me how you got on with the car yards."

As soon as the words were out of her mouth Blondie could feel her face reddening.

*God, how bloody obvious! Why did I say that? He must know a phone call would have been enough.*

But before she could say anything else, Chris gave her a smile that nearly made her knees buckle.

"That sounds absolutely essential to the investigation Detective Green." The smile stayed on his face. "You know the Southern Cross?"

"I used to spend quite a bit of time there when I was younger. They've done it up I believe?"

"Yeah, the garden bar's great now."

"Around eight suit you? I doubt I'll finish any earlier."

"Sounds like a plan. You have my cell. Give me a call if you get held up."

Blondie handed Chris the list. "Will do."

She watched Chris as he walked towards the lifts. At least she'd have something to daydream about while she made phone calls today.

**********

Gerard had gotten up early. Today he was playing the role of Chris Thompson, builder, and wanted to allow himself enough time to get to the empty section opposite the school gate before 8:00 a.m. After a quick shower, he had a line of speed and a cup of coffee for breakfast.

"100% fat and cholesterol free," he joked to himself. He felt great, wide-awake, energized, and ready for anything. Wearing his builder's outfit, he made his way downstairs. After climbing into the van he fastened his seatbelt and glanced at his watch.

"Time for work Mr. Thompson!"

When Gerard arrived in Mount Victoria, he parked opposite the unused school gate. He opened the van's sliding door, and took his tool-belt, fastening it around his waist. A bright orange vest and white hard-hat completed his disguise. With pad and pencil in hand, Gerard walked onto the empty section and started measuring the distance between the various pegs, pretending to do work in preparation for the foundations being poured. He wrote the measurements on the top page of the pad. On the second page, out of view, he took his real notes, the important stuff. What the teachers were wearing, what time the various households in the area left for work, anything that might impact on his plans.

It wasn't long before people started moving about as they started their day. Cars drove up and down the street as people headed off to work. At 8:02 a.m. a man and a woman, both dressed in typical corporate attire, drove out of their garage and disappeared to the left. At 8:05 a.m. three young people who looked like university students came out of a two-flat property up the road, and strolled past him heading towards town. Gerard made a note for each movement. In a house up the road, a man left at 8:10 a.m. At 8:15 a.m. another man came out a house two doors down, walked past him, crossed the street, turned left, and disappeared around the corner. The man looked like a teacher, probably from Redford School judging by his suit. Then by 8:20 a.m. the neighbourhood was quiet again.

After a brief lull, schoolchildren started to arrive and traffic around the school picked up again. Some students arrived on foot, but most were driven by parents.

When he looked across the street, Gerard could see children milling about in the school yard waiting for classes to start.

At 8:35 a.m. Ashna Patel walked by with Tapiwa, and Heather, two of the girls that played with her in the school orchestra. A minute later, James Warner and his mother drove past. James waved to the girls out the window. Not one of them took any notice of Gerard.

By 8:50 a.m. boys and girls were running around the schoolyard or sitting in groups talking as they waited for the bell to ring. Gerard noticed a boy and a girl near the gate talking, heads close together. The young girl he recognised. She was one of the three who'd walked past him earlier. Then when the bell rang at five minutes to nine, the students went inside, and the school grounds were suddenly deserted.

Having done what he came to do, Gerard decided to pack it in and returned to the van. It all looked good from his point of view, especially the fact that some of the children played near the gate. This spot had lots of potential. It was time for him to get to work. He had a lot of preparation to do. Then with a bit of luck, tomorrow would be a day for everyone to remember.

# CHAPTER 9 - THURSDAY AFTERNOON

After leaving the school, Gerard spent his time getting the van ready for the next day. He turned the crate onto its side, and bolted it to the floor opposite the van's sliding door. He planned to use the crate's lid and some wooden blocks mounted to the crate to form a sliding door. Then once he'd fitted a latch, Gerard would be able to shove a child in the crate and lock it quickly from the outside. Timing was everything, and speed essential. This simple but effective method of capture and concealment had worked before.

Gerard glued and screwed a layer of polystyrene insulation and an extra sheet of plywood onto the outside of the crate. When the kid started screaming, and they always did, this extra layer of soundproofing, combined with the van's stereo being turned up, would muffle their cries for help.

On the top of the crate, he stacked half a dozen lengths of timber, before filling the back of the van with his props. A few scraps of timber, some tools, and a couple of empty boxes completed the illusion.

Next Gerard assembled the camp stretchers. To keep his captive for any length of time he'd need a place for them to sleep. He would need the occasional nap too. Playing could be incredibly tiring at times.

By the time Gerard had completed these tasks, it was nearly 3:00 p.m. Children would be heading home from school soon. He decided to have one last drive around Redford School, map out the safest route from the school to the workshop, and look for escape routes along the way in the event something went wrong. Gerard knew from experience that it never hurt to have options.

Chris and Andy knocked off work at 5.00 p.m. Police work was often a numbers game, and getting used to disappointment came with the territory. The old saying, 'you always find what you're searching for in the last place you look' might be true but it didn't make things any less frustrating. They hadn't managed to visit all of the car dealers on the list Blondie had given them because they still had their own work to get through, but they'd made a fair dent in it. Still, it had been a disappointing day, and their lack of sleep the previous night had caught up with them.

Andy was keen to get home. He had a hot date with a bowl of chilli con carne and the final episode of *The Sopranos*. A big fan from the beginning Andy was looking forward to finding out what happened to Tony Soprano and his family. His excitement had an undertone of sadness at the series ending. Thursday nights wouldn't be the same without it.

Chris headed home to his small cottage in Brooklyn for a quick nap and a shower, before his meeting with Blondie at eight. After parking his car out front, he walked up a short path and climbed the three steps which led onto a veranda, still bathed in afternoon sun.

For a moment Chris turned and looked out at the city below with its bush-clad hills and sparkling harbour. From Chris's place high on the Brooklyn hill, Wellington looked like a picture postcard on a good day. On a stormy day however, with the wind howling and the rain thrashing, the city could disappear under the clouds altogether.

After his nap, Chris put on his favourite jeans and cotton shirt, and then checked himself in the mirror.

Being such a nice evening, and knowing he'd have a few drinks, Chris decided to leave his car at home and walk down the bush track that meandered through the green belt into town. Some light exercise and fresh air were just what he needed to relax before his meeting with Blondie.

As Chris entered the Southern Cross, he took a quick peek at his watch. He was ten minutes early. After passing a few tables and the unlit fireplace, Chris headed towards the main bar on the left. He couldn't see Blondie anywhere, so he ordered a lager and made his way through the French doors into the garden area at the rear of the premises.

Strings of lights gave the garden a festive feel and

Wellington's wind was still off having a holiday in the Bahamas somewhere. It surprised Chris that the garden bar was only half-full on such a nice night, but then he remembered it was only Thursday after all. Tomorrow would be a different story. He located an empty booth that was relatively private, yet still allowed him a view inside, and waited.

Blondie walked in a few minutes later. She was wearing a brightly printed skirt, silk blouse, and red belt that accentuated her lovely curves. Red sandals and matching bag completed the ensemble. Chris was surprised at how the colour suited her. The outfit was far more flattering that the plain blue uniform she wore to work.

Blondie spotted Chris through the window and waved. She ordered a glass of Chardonnay and then came outside to join Chris.

"Hey there Detective Spacey," Blondie said with a smile.

"Hey there Detective Green," Chris mimicked, smiling back at her.

Expecting Blondie to sit opposite him in the booth, Chris got a pleasant surprise when she slid into the booth beside him.

"So how'd you guys go with the car yards?"

Her closeness distracted him. She smelled good, like lavender with a hint of something Chris couldn't quite distinguish. As he inhaled slowly, Chris realised Blondie was waiting for an answer. "Well," Chris said reaching into his pocket, "we got through a fair few of them. No luck so far, but we'll finish the last one first thing in the morning." He put the list on the table. All but one entry had lines drawn through them. "We've also been showing Williamson's picture around when we've had the opportunity."

"Hey thanks again for doing this." Blondie turned her head to look directly at him. "It makes a big difference."

As Chris gazed into her lovely brown eyes he felt his cock twitch. "So how'd you and Warner go, any new information?"

"Nothing except more vans to check out. There are 52 potentials now, less those we eliminated today. That still leaves around 30. Warner said we might have to expand the search to include Porirua and the Kapiti Coast. Maybe even up the line as far as Otaki or Levin if nothing turns up soon. The worst thing is we're not even sure he's bought a van."

"How's the canvassing going?" Chris asked. "If he's local someone must have seen him. A supermarket, dairy, petrol station ..."

"We've enlisted more manpower, and expanded the canvas, but Warner's still determined to press on searching for a van. He's convinced that's the key. I'm not sure what I think any more."

But Blondie knew very well what she was thinking. She was thinking how sexy Chris was and wondering what it would be like to feel his skin against hers. She also wondered if it was wise to start something with a man from work. 'No' would be her normal reaction. Besides, she was in the middle of a major investigation.

"So," Chris said. "Now that we've got the work stuff out of the way, would you like to have a bite to eat or should we skip the meal and go straight home to bed."

Blondie's eyebrows creased briefly, wondering which way to take his comment. Did he mean go home together or separately? Then she saw his huge smile and twinkling eyes. Ah, a joke. But was it?

Composing herself, Blondie slid closer to Chris. She leaned in, placing a hand on his forearm, before whispering in a low and sexy voice, "Bed sounds good big fella, but how about we have a bite first." And with that she nipped the lobe of his left ear.

This time, it was Chris's turn to be surprised. When he looked into Blondie's eyes he could see them shining, a smile plastered across her face. "Ouch!" Chris said, rubbing his ear, pretending to be in pain. "That hurt so good you bad girl. Any more of that behaviour and I'll have to put you in handcuffs."

Blondie giggled like a schoolgirl. "Help us catch Williamson, and I might just let you."

**********

It was just after 11:00 p.m. Gerard had one little job to do under the cover of darkness. The drive from his apartment to the school would only take 10 minutes at this time of night.

When he pulled up outside the old gate of Redford School, he positioned the van with two wheels on the footpath so it would obscure the gate from any night owls in the street should they look in his direction. Grabbing his recently purchased bolt cutters he cut off the gate's padlock, and replaced it with one of his own. The new padlock he'd scratched and dirtied up in the workshop. After snapping it onto the chain, it looked as though it had been there forever. Then he took a small container of oil, and put a couple big squirts on each of the gate's hinges, working them back and forth a few times to make sure they'd open silently when the time came.

It was all so easy. In less than two minutes the job was finished and Gerard was on his way home to bed.

*I need my sleep. It's going to be big day tomorrow.*

# CHAPTER 10 - FRIDAY MORNING

By 8:00 a.m. Gerard was dressed and out the door. He hadn't felt this excited since the day he grabbed the Bourne kid. As he jumped into the driver's seat and started the van, he ran through a mental list of things he'd discovered the previous day.

The best news was that there had been a couple of children near the old gate prior to school starting. With luck, that would be the case again today. However, too many children at the same time could present problems. The fewer kids around when he made his move, the less chance he had of getting noticed. The last thing he needed was for a bunch of screeching kids to raise the alarm. Besides, one playmate was all he needed.

Gerard had also discovered how the teachers at Redford School dressed. So today he was dressed in a similar fashion, wearing dark blue trousers, white shirt, dark blue tie, and black shoes. There wouldn't be a school crest on his tie, but the one he'd taken from the lawyer was near enough. A child wouldn't notice a small detail like that ... not in time anyway.

There had only been two teachers monitoring the play area the previous day, and both had stayed close to the main building at the opposite end of the field. If that was the case again today, the teachers would be nearly 100 metres away if and when Gerard made his move.

Gerard turned on the radio and sang along to the music as he drove towards Redford School.

When he arrived, he parked the van as close as he could to the gate. Then, before too many people started moving about, he unlocked the gate in readiness, leaving the padlock hooked on the chain to create the illusion it was still fastened.

Plan A was to grab a child as they walked past the van on their way to school, toss them into the crate, and drive away, but this scenario depended on who was in the street at the time.

If no opportunity presented itself outside the school, Plan B was to wait until one of the children in the schoolyard came near the gate. Then he'd quickly slip onto the school grounds, do his teacher impersonation, and manoeuvre them to the gate. Once he'd done that, he could drag them into his waiting van. Relocking the gate would stop the teachers from following even if he had been noticed. Then, before anyone could do a thing he'd be gone.

Gerard looked at his watch. It was nearly time. A familiar tingle of excitement coursed through his body. The early birds would be arriving soon.

Alert in the driver's seat with a newspaper across the steering wheel, and an old checked work-shirt buttoned over the top of his white shirt, Gerard pretended to read. A disguise was always better than trying to hide, he'd discovered. To anyone passing, he looked like a builder having a quick read of the paper before starting work. Hiding in plain sight had worked before.

Sneaking a glance into the side mirror, Gerard noticed a mother hand in hand with her son walking his way. She didn't even look at him. To her he was invisible, which was just the way he liked it.

*********

James Warner and his mother, Julia, left the house a little earlier than usual. Julia had a dental appointment in town at 9:00 a.m. so she needed to drop James off well before that if she was going to make it on time.

During breakfast, Robert Warner had asked his wife to make sure she delivered James to the school's main entrance and watch him until he was safely on school property. "There's no point in taking risks honey."

Julia agreed without hesitation.

Robert Warner looked over to where his son was crunching his way through a large bowl of cereal. "James, I want you to stay inside the school grounds until one of us comes to pick you up this afternoon. James, do you hear me?

James nodded in response wondering what the big deal was all about.

Robert reached out and gently lifted his son's chin up, looking into his eyes. "Absolutely no exceptions. Got it?"

After the short drive, Julia pulled up outside the school. James hopped out of the car and jogged off, anxious to see if Ashna had arrived. Then, with James safely delivered, Julia drove off down the hill towards the city.

Getting to school early was fine with James. It would allow him more time to spend with Ashna before class. If time permitted, they usually went to their favourite spot at the far end of the playing field where there was some privacy. They were both keen amateur scientists and often worked on little projects together away from the noise and chaos of the other students.

**********

Ashna Patel left home at 8:15 a.m. It would only take her 10 minutes or so to walk the four blocks to Redford School. Dressed in her school uniform and carrying her blue knapsack with its picture of Albert Einstein emblazoned on it, she took her mother's hand as they headed down the driveway. Ashna hummed the song she'd learned in music class the day before.

For the first block, Ashna and her mother walked in the same direction. Then, at the first intersection, Ashna's mother turned down the hill towards town, leaving her daughter to walk the last few blocks on her own.

Ashna was looking forward to seeing James. She'd overheard her older brothers talking about some weird guy who'd escaped from prison. She didn't quite understand a couple of things they'd said and was hoping James could clear the matter up for her.

Ashna had an inquisitive mind and wanted to know virtually everything about anything. Naturally curious, she would often look up new words in the dictionary. If she wanted to know more about a topic, she'd find more information in the school library, or on the internet. She also liked to double check that what people told her was true. People often repeated things they'd been told without bothering to verify that what they were passing on was correct.

If she was going to be a scientist when she grew up, she needed to make sure she checked her facts. Check, check and re-check her science teacher had told her. Never assume anything.

**********

Gerard watched the growing numbers of pupils arrive at the school. Many were dropped off by their parents. Some walked past with adults or in groups, but none so far had appeared by themselves. Still, it was only 8:20 a.m. There were plenty more to come.

Then in his rear vision mirror, Gerard noticed a brown skinned girl wearing a Redford School uniform turn the corner. She was alone, and heading in his direction. He looked around to see if anyone else was about, and smiled when he saw the street was empty. He stiffened slightly. If he was going to grab her, he'd have to make a decision in the next thirty seconds.

Gerard folded the newspaper, dropped it on to the passenger seat, and climbed out of the van. He went around to the side door, and slid it open. His head pivoted left, then right. The street was still empty. Was this the opportunity he'd been waiting for? It was decision time.

*Let the games begin.*

The girl was only ten seconds away. Gerard slid the crate door open in readiness. Ten, nine, eight, seven, six ... Then a door slammed.

When Gerard looked up towards the noise, he saw that a man had come out of the house across the street and was walking directly towards him.

*What the hell?*

"Hi Mr. Jackaways," the girl called out. She was only five metres from the van now.

*Fuck, fuck, fuck!*

Gerard closed the crate again and leaned into the van.

"Hi Ashna," the man said in reply. "You're early for school."

The man was only metres away now. He walked just behind the van towards the girl. Gerard grabbed the carpenter's tool belt, and clipped it around his waist. Then reaching for a few tools, he pretended to be getting ready to start work. Gerard turned his face away from the two pedestrians as they neared.

"I love school." Ashna said with a grin, falling in step beside the man.

Gerard heard the girl's voice directly behind him. Not daring to turn around, he continued to fiddle with his props in the back of the van.

"Nice to see a young lady who likes school more than Play Station or T.V." Gerard heard the man say. "While we walk, why don't you tell me what you learned at school yesterday."

They were past him now, their voices retreating down the road. Gerard turned and watched their backs as they continued on their way, exhaling a big breath. Gerard realised his hands were shaking slightly. He wiped his sleeve across the beads of sweat on his brow.

"I could sing you a song," Ashna said, and without waiting for a reply, she started into her rendition of *All Creatures Great and Small.*

Gerard kicked a tyre and cursed his bad luck as the singing faded.

*Fuck, fuck, fuck!*

Once the girl and the teacher turned the corner, Gerard unbuckled the tool belt and threw it into the back of the van, closed the door, and returned to the driver's seat.

*Shit that was close.*

"Thanks Mr. Jackaways," Ashna said once they'd reached the school's entrance.

"My pleasure young lady, I'll see you in class at nine."

"I'll be there," Ashna said before skipping off along the path and up the short flight of steps that led into the school's main building.

Inside the building, long hallways lead off in both directions. A cacophony of noise bounced off the corridor walls as the students prepared to start their day. The building was shaped like a wide U with a small courtyard in its centre. A brick wall, attached to each end of the U enclosed the rest of the school grounds, forming a rectangle that covered a complete city block.

Continuing straight ahead, Ashna walked through the building and out through the double doors leading into the courtyard. There, sitting on a wooden bench waiting for her, was James Warner.

"Hey you beat me to school today," Ashna said looking down at her best friend.

"My mum had a dentist appointment this morning so she dropped me off early. Hey, I've brought my mouse in to show you. I think you'll find its behaviour rather interesting."

Ashna's eyes brightened. "Cool."

Ashna followed James as he walked out onto the playground, heading for the far end of the field near the old gate. The other children running and screeching would have made it too hard to hear each other if they'd stayed where they were. Besides, they liked their privacy.

Once she'd had a chance to a look at James's mouse, Ashna would ask James to explain what her brothers had been talking about.

**********

Fewer students were arriving now so Gerard got out of the van and peered through the bars of the gate. Then he scanned the street. There were no other pedestrians around, and the traffic had dwindled away. It was time for plan B.

He knew he couldn't afford to hang around for long. If someone noticed him loitering, they might get suspicious and ring the cops.

Most of the children Gerard could see were at the other end of the playground. A couple of boys were tossing a rugby ball back and forth out in the middle, but they were still 30 metres away. One of the male teachers looked young and reasonably fit. If Gerard ventured too far onto the playing field and the teacher noticed him, he may not have time to get back to the gate, especially dragging a struggling child. Gerard didn't gamble unless he was confident he knew what the outcome would be.

He'd only survived this long by not taking silly chances.

As he began to think today's efforts were going to be a washout, Gerard noticed two kids emerge from the pack and start walking in his direction. Stepping back behind the wall, hiding himself from view, he waited a few seconds, and then peeked through the gate again.

The boy and girl were only twenty metres away now, both with their heads down looking at something the boy had in his hand, a small cardboard box by the looks of it. The box's lid was up, and they were both peering inside with great interest. Every step they took brought them closer. He might have a chance after all.

*Come on you little beauties.*

Gerard waited another 10 seconds, and then looked again. They were really close now.

*Which one should I go for?*

Hurrying back to the van, he opened the side door, then reached in and slid back the door of the crate. He took off the work shirt and threw it inside, revealing his teacher's outfit beneath.

It was time to make a decision.

*The boy or the girl?*

Ashna and James had almost reached the gate before veering slightly right and disappearing from view. Gerard could still hear them talking excitedly, so he knew they hadn't gone far. They must be right along the inside of the wall. So close.

Gerard unhooked the chain and opened the gate slowly. The oil on the hinges had done the trick. The ruckus made by the other kids on the playground hid what little sound the gate made as it swung outward. Gerard looked up and down the street one last time, and then checked that the teachers on the far side of the playing field were still looking elsewhere. They were so busy chatting, they were oblivious to Gerard as he stepped through the gate. When Gerard looked to the left, the boy and the girl were sitting on the ground opposite each other, legs crossed, with heads close together. Both were fascinated by the box lying on the ground between them. They were deep in conversation as the boy played with whatever was inside, totally engrossed. Neither child had heard him enter. They were miles away in their own private bubble, smiles on their faces. Gerard took a few steps forward stopping a few metres short of where the two children were sitting.

"Excuse me you two. Get up and come here please," Gerard said in a kind but stern voice.

Ashna and James looked up in surprise. They'd been so focused on what they were doing they hadn't heard him approach. Ashna grabbed the box, quickly closing its lid. Then getting to their feet, the children slowly approached him.

"You," Gerard said, indicating the girl, "Come with me please." He took Ashna's hand in his, turned, and started walking the few metres back towards the gate, guiding her gently along beside him.

Ashna was confused. She didn't recognise this teacher. "What's the matter, did I do something wrong?"

"No, nothing's the matter. Just come with me a moment. I'll explain."

But Ashna wanted an explanation now, not later. With his hand firmly clamped around her wrist, Gerard's pull became more insistent as Ashna resisted. The box slipped from her grasp as she tried to stop the man from pulling her along.

As Ashna and the man moved closer to the gate, James bent down, picked up the box, and thrust it deep into his pocket. Then he moved forward again, staying a few metres behind them.

When Gerard reached the gate, he looked out. No one was in the street. Gerard turned toward James. "You stay there. Don't worry we'll be back in a minute."

Once outside the gate, the man's tug was stronger. Ashna didn't want to go with this teacher without some explanation.

"Where are we going?" she asked, digging her heels in.

Gerard's answered with a sharp tug that nearly pulled Ashna off her feet. A squeal escaped her mouth as she lost her footing, the toes of her shoes scraping the pavement as the man dragged her along. When she regained her balance and looked up, she realized the man was dragging her towards the open door of a van. He wasn't a teacher at all.

"James! Help me!"

James was almost at the gate when he heard Ashna's scream. He ran to see what was happening. The man had pushed Ashna into a wooden box, and was in the process of closing the door.

"Stop!" James yelled as he ran towards Gerard, wrapping his arms around Gerard's leg. Gerard backhanded the boy in the side of the head, knocking him to the ground. Then he latched the crate's door on the screaming girl.

When Gerard looked back at the boy, he was starting to get up. Then Gerard's mind clicked. He looked up and down the street once again. There was not a soul in sight.

*It must be my lucky day.*

Gerard grabbed James around the waist with one arm, lifting him off the ground. The boy struggled, squirming and twisting, arms flailing, but Gerard was too strong. In one fluid motion, Gerard slid the door of the crate back and tossed James in on top of Ashna.

The force of James's body knocked Ashna flat. She yelped in pain. Gerard quickly closed the crate, and latched the door again, leaving them in darkness.

Gerard ran back to the gate, wrapped the chain around the bars, and heard a solid click as the padlock engaged. When he got back to the van, he heard the muffled sound of the two children yelling and pounding on the inside of the plywood walls.

Glancing first into the schoolyard where the two teachers were still deep in conversation, and then up and down the street, Gerard allowed himself a big grin as he realised that no one had seen a thing.

*It's all in the timing.*

Gerard walked calmly around the van and climbed into the driver's seat, started the engine, and turned up the stereo. Now he had everything he needed. Half way down the street, he checked the rear-view mirror. The street was empty.

As he drove, Gerard hummed along to the music, thinking of the bonus he'd scored.

*Two playmates for the price of one!*

**********

"Ashna Patel." Mr. Jackaways called out, his eyes looking down at the list of students on the desktop in front of him. "Ashna Patel?" Looking up at the faces in the classroom, the teacher couldn't see Ashna. "Has anyone seen Ashna? I know she's here at school, I saw her earlier."

The other students shook their heads, so Jackaways continued calling out names.

A minute later Jackaways called out, "James Warner."

There was no reply.

"James are you here?" When Jackaways looked up, he could see James was missing as well. "Billy, go out and see if you can find James and Ashna. If they're not on the playground, pop into the office, and see if Mrs. Wilkinson knows where they are."

A few minutes later Billy was back. "They're not outside Mr Jackaways. Mrs. Wilkinson hasn't seen them either.

After finishing roll call and having a moment's thought about the missing students Jackaways stood up from his desk. "Class, I need to pop out for a moment. Work on your geography assignment while I'm gone. Tapiwa you're in charge. I'll be back as soon as I can. Okay now ... heads down and get to work."

As he walked down the hallway towards the office, Jackaways wondered what those two rascals were doing. Surely, they couldn't be far away.

"Mrs. Wilkinson," Jackaways said as he entered the office. "I seem to be missing two students, James Warner and Ashna Patel. I know they were here earlier. Would you please put a call out over the intercom and ask them to come to the office?"

"Sure, no problem, I'll do it now."

Mrs Wilkinson grabbed the microphone from the corner of her desk. "Ashna Patel and James Warner, please report to the office. Ashna Patel and James Warner, please report to the office." She turned back toward Jackaways. "There, that should do the trick."

They both waited. After five minutes passed with no sign of

Ashna and James, Jackaways had a worried look on his face. "Would you try again? This is most unusual."

"Ashna Patel and James Warner please report to the office immediately! Ashna Patel and James Warner please report to the office immediately!"

**********

Chris and Andy's first job of the morning had just been completed. They'd just returned to their car after showing Gerard's picture to a salesman at the Toyota dealership on Kent Terrace, the last one on their list, when a call came through on the radio reporting the two missing pupils from Redford School.

They looked at each other, "Are you thinking what I'm thinking?" Chris said as started the car.

Andy nodded. "Let's just hope it's a false alarm. Kids wag school all the time."

"Shit I hope so."

Andy grabbed the radio. "Only one way to find out." He pushed the transmit button. "DC12 responding. ETA Redford School five minutes."

"Copy DC12."

Andy flipped the switch for the lights and siren as Chris swung out onto Cambridge Terrace and pushed his foot hard down on the accelerator.

Minutes later they came to a screeching halt outside the school.

Jackaways heard the car arrive. When the two police officers climb out and walk briskly towards the entrance, he came out to meet them at the top of the steps.

"Oh thank god you're here. Two of my students have disappeared. We've searched the entire school but can't find them anywhere!"

"When was the last time they were seen?" Andy asked.

"They were both on the playground before the bell rang for first period. That was 10 or 15 minutes before nine."

"So about 45 minutes ago. Okay. Can you give me their names

and a description?" Andy pulled a small notebook from his back pocket.

"The girl's name is Ashna Patel, age twelve, long dark hair, olive skin, of Indian descent. The boy is James Warner. He's the same age, blond, and fair-skinned. One of the women in the office is looking for a photo of them now."

"James Warner you say?" Chris asked Jackaways. "Is his dad a police officer by any chance?"

"Yes, I believe so. Do you know him?"

"Yeah I know him," Chris said, his stomach churning.

"They're both very good pupils. It's not like them to miss class. Oh God this is terrible."

"Don't worry Mr....?"

"Jackaways, Jason Jackaways. I'm deputy principal here at Redford."

"Okay Mr. Jackaways, try not to worry," Chris said. "You haven't seen anything unusual recently, anyone hanging around the school in the last day or two by any chance? Driving a van perhaps?"

"Not that I can remember ... no wait, on second thought, I saw a white van when I walked to work this morning. How did you know there would be a van?"

Chris ignored his question. "So, where exactly was this van you saw?"

"It was by the old gate at the far end of the playground," Jackaways replied. "A builder I think. There was a name on the side of the van, but for the life of me I can't remember what it was."

"Don't worry about that now Mr. Jackaways," what else can you tell us about this builder?" Chris asked.

"Well, when I passed him he looked like he was getting ready for work. I thought at the time he must be working on those new town houses they're building a couple of doors down from where I live. Shit! Now that you mention it, I saw the same van there yesterday. He was measuring foundations as I walked past."

"Did you get a look at him by any chance?" Andy asked.

"Not his face, he was turned the other way. He was wearing a work shirt, average height and weight I'd say. I must admit I didn't take much notice. Do you think he might be involved with James and Ashna disappearance?"

"It's a possibility, but let's not jump to conclusions." Chris turned to Andy, "Hey let's get some reinforcements up here and start combing the neighbourhood. Radio the station and let them know what's going on will you."

"I'm on it," Andy said over his shoulder, already turning to head back to their car.

Chris looked at Jackaways. "Let's go see if your colleague has found those photos shall we? The sooner those are distributed, the sooner we'll find James and Ashna."

*And we'd better find them fast, especially if Gerard has the poor little buggers.*

**********

Ashna and James had given up yelling. Their throats were sore and their ears rang from all the noise they'd been making in the confined space of the crate. The ride had been uncomfortable, bouncing them around every time the van hit a bump in the road. Both were feeling a bit bruised and battered from contact with the hard floor. Ashna was crying softly.

"We'll be okay," James said as he rubbed the side of his face.

"I'm … I'm scared James. Where is he taking us?" Ashna turned towards James, but in the darkness of the crate, she could only see a vague shape.

"I don't know, but remember my Dad's a policeman. He'll do something. Just keep calm."

They'd only been in the crate for fifteen minutes, but it felt much, much longer. It was stinking hot, with only the slightest amount of light and air entering the cracks around the door. The two of them sat side by side, their backs against the plywood wall, knees up to their chests. James could feel Ashna trembling.

"Don't cry Ashna, we'll be okay." He put his arm around Ashna's shoulders and felt her lean towards him.

Gerard hummed to the music as he drove down Aotea Quay towards the motorway on-ramp that would take him out to Petone. Traffic had been heavy, and he'd had a bad run with the lights. Road works had sprung up overnight opposite the Michael Fowler Centre narrowing three lanes to one, creating a tangle of vehicles as they squeezed past the trucks and workmen. Another five minutes and he'd be on the motorway. Then after 10 minutes or so on the motorway he'd be safe. He didn't have long to go now.

As he drove, Gerard wondered if the police had found the car he'd stolen from the prison yet. He doubted it. He'd read somewhere that thousands of cars were stolen every year, and the cops only recover 30 percent of them.

Fifteen minutes later, Gerard indicated and turned left into Cornish Street. Half way along the street, he triggered the remote control and pulled the van inside. As Gerard heard the door close behind him, a long sigh escaped his lips.

*Well done Mr Williamson!*

**********

"What!" Warner shouted into his cell phone. "What do you mean James is missing?"

"We're at his school now," Chris said, holding the phone further from his ear. "Seems he and a girl named Ashna Patel didn't show up for class this morning. When the teachers couldn't find them, they called the police. Andy and I took the call."

"Fuck Chris, tell me this isn't happening."

"We've already got three units scouring the neighbourhood with current photos, and a canine unit is on its way. With any luck they've just gone walkabout."

"I hope you're right, but somehow I doubt it. I don't think James would have left the school. Especially after the lecture I gave him this morning about how he wasn't to leave the school grounds until Julia or I picked him up. He's a good boy. I don't think he'd blatantly disobey me."

Chris knew all twelve-year-olds disobeyed their parents some of the time. He certainly had. But what Chris really dreaded telling Warner, was what they'd discovered about the van.

"There is one bit of unsettling news, and I'm not sure how to say this without worrying you unnecessarily but," Chris said, taking a deep breath, "the deputy principal saw a white van parked by a disused gate at the far end of the school this morning. Said it was a tradesmen's van. Had a name on the side, so it could be legit, but there's no sign of it now."

"Did anyone get the name on the van? Have you checked it out?" Warner asked, praying he'd wake up and discover he was having a nightmare.

"No not yet. Once we've finished canvassing the neighbourhood we might know more. None of the patrols have seen a van fitting the description in the area so far."

"Please find my boy."

"We'll do everything we can, believe me sir."

"Blondie and I are in the Hutt. We'll be with you as soon as we can."

"Okay. Andy and I are going to start knocking on doors around the school."

"Check the school's gate too," Warner said. "Williamson might have used it to gain access. Remember he grabbed the Bourne boy from a playground."

"Will do Sir."

Warner turned to Blondie and explained the situation as they walked quickly towards the car. Within minutes they were racing along the motorway.

When the speedometer reached 140kph Blondie started to freak out. "Would you please slow down, you're not going to be of much use to your son if you're killed on the motorway. Besides, I don't feel like becoming a statistic today."

If Warner had heard her, he wasn't taking any notice. It was a white-knuckled ride into town with lights flashing and siren blaring the whole way. Twenty minutes later, they skidded to a halt behind Andy and Chris's car. The two detectives were on the front porch of a house talking to a woman. As Warner and

Blondie got out of the car, Chris closed his notebook and turned around. He had a look on his face Blondie hadn't seen before. Chris nodded an acknowledgement in Warner and Blondie's direction as he started towards them.

At the far end of the street, Blondie noticed another officer standing beside a police car, talking to an elderly man on the footpath. The officer was holding up, what Blondie assumed was a photograph. At least the troops were arriving in numbers now.

"So anything?" Warner asked.

"You were right about the gate," Chris said. "The padlock's been swapped."

"Fuck!" Warner yelled, hands shooting to his head and closing over his ears as if to keep the bad news out.

"I hate to say this, but there's another reason to worry."

"What's that?" Warner asked, afraid of what he was about to hear.

"Well, Mrs. Tate, the lady we've just been speaking to, said she remembers seeing a van yesterday at the building site and then again this morning parked near the gate. Seems she goes to her sister's place most mornings. Anyway, she remembers the name on the van."

"What was it?" Warner asked.

"Chris Thompson Construction," Chris said bracing himself.

"Why is that a problem?" asked Warner, as his eyes narrowed and brow folded into horizontal lines.

"Well, I'm Chris," Chris said. Then he pointed towards his colleague. "And he's Andy Thompson. It's too much of a coincidence considering the fingers and all."

"Bloody hell," Warner said, the colour draining from his face.

"We have to assume Gerard's snatched the kids. Using our names on the van is Gerard playing some twisted game. He thinks he's clever."

"Yeah, he gave us the finger when he killed his dad too," Blondie added. "Have you informed the Patel family yet?"

"There's a constable on the way to them now," Chris replied. "As hard as this may seem Sir, I think you and Blondie should keep at it. You know, trying to track down the van through the dealers. There's no point hanging around here, this end is well and truly covered. We should keep working this from as many angles as we can, don't you think? Then one of them might pay off."

"I think Chris is right," Blondie said. "Let's get back to work and track down that van. Find that, we'll find the kids. We'll just get in the way here. Not much point in going over the same ground is there?"

Warner, his eyes downcast, could see their logic. Even so, the thought of leaving the scene distressed him.

"Here, give me the keys," Blondie said, her hand held out towards Warner. "You can ring Julia while I drive us back to the station." There was no way Blondie wanted Warner behind the wheel in his current state. One white-knuckle ride a day was more than sufficient.

Warner rubbed his temple with his fingers. "What a fucking mess."

"I'll give you a call later to compare notes Detective Spacey," Blondie said.

Chris smiled despite the gravity of the situation as he remembered their meeting last night, and the kiss she'd given him as they left the pub. His gaze lingered on Blondie as she guided Warner by the elbow to the passenger side of their car.

Andy nudged Chris in the ribs. "Okay mate, enough daydreaming. Let's get moving and catch this crazy bastard."

**********

Once back at the workshop, Gerard took the two children out of the crate and locked them into the back room. He'd had a bit of trouble with the boy, having to drag the feisty little chap, kicking and screaming the whole way.

As much as Gerard would have loved some fun right away, there were chores he had to do first. One was removing the sign-writing from the van so he could drive it again.

The lettering took almost as long to get off, as is had to put on.

"Should have chosen a shorter name" Gerard said to himself

as he carefully peeled each letter off the side of the van and removed the adhesive residue with turps. Still the name had served its purpose. Gerard loved playing mind games with the cops.

After the van was anonymous once again, and ready for use when required, Gerard praised himself for his excellent choice of vehicle. It had run like a dream.

*Good old Japanese reliability.*

Next, Gerard cleaned out the van's interior. Unbolting the crate, he dragged it out of the van and pushed it up against the wall under the work bench out of the way. The other props were stacked beside the crate. The lengths of timber he left on the floor to one side.

It took just under two hours for Gerard to finish his housekeeping. As he worked he thought about the things he would do to his captives. He was in no rush. Anticipation was often the best part, and now that he had a private place, he could take all the time he liked. First he'd do a line of speed, and then it would be decision time.

*The boy or the girl?*

**********

James and Ashna had been sitting on the floor in the back room, their backs to the wall, for what seemed like ages. James checked his watch. It was almost noon. He'd been looking around the room trying to figure out a way to escape, but had come up blank. He got up and tried the door. It was locked of course, bolted from the other side. James looked down at Ashna. Her eyes were red and puffy. The man made him so angry. With fists clenched, James kicked the wall in frustration.

Not knowing what else to do, James decided to check out the cabinets under the sink. Behind the first door, he discovered a few old plates, some cups and saucers, three teaspoons, and a bottle of dishwashing liquid. Finding nothing else he could use as a weapon, James grabbed one of the spoons. Clutching the spoon in his fist, he made a series of stabbing motions before putting it back. Stabbing someone four times your size with a spoon was a silly idea he concluded. It would just piss the guy off.

"What are you doing?" Ashna whispered. "Don't let him catch you, he might hit you again."

"I'm just trying to find a weapon, so we can protect ourselves," James explained.

The next cupboard was empty except for a cockroach. James brought his fist down on it, spreading it flat on the shelf, a small blotch of roach guts oozing out. After wiping his hand on his pants, he pulled open the next door. There was food sitting on the shelf, tins of spaghetti, baked beans, and a couple jars of chilli peppers.

Behind the last door, sitting on the middle shelf, was a first aid kit, a bottle of disinfectant and two rolls of gauze bandage. Opening the first aid kit James found band-aids, eye wash, some aspirin, and a small pair of scissors. The scissors he slipped into his pocket.

After finding nothing of use in the bathroom, James returned to the main room and sat down by Ashna again, his eyes still darting around the room in search of something that might help them escape.

He was scared, but for Ashna's sake James was determined to tough it out. He leaned into Ashna and put his arm over her shoulder.

A moment later James felt Ashna tense up.

"I hear footsteps," she whispered. "He's coming."

**********

Having snorted a couple lines of speed, Gerard was buzzing. He unlocked the door to find the two kids sitting on the floor. The girl looked up with a frightened expression, leaning towards the boy for protection. The boy glared up with undisguised hatred.

Gerard looked them over with a critical eye. The tingling sensation running through his body was half speed, half anticipation.

*The boy or the girl? The girl looks like she might be fun. Yes the girl. Just a finger, then he could test out the boy. See how tough he really is.*

"What's your name?" Gerard asked, looking at the girl.

Ashna said nothing, hiding her face in her arms instead.

Gerard could see the girl shaking.

"Her name is Ashna, and I'm James," the boy said looking him straight in the eye. "My father's a policeman. He's going to put you in jail for doing this mister, so you'd better let us go."

"A policeman eh? Well James, now isn't that interesting? So what's your last name then?"

"Warner," James said defiantly.

"So your father would be Detective Inspector Robert Warner would he?"

"How ... how did you know that?"

"I'm an old friend of your father. In fact, I might even send him a jar of my favourite chillies very soon," Gerard said, chuckling to himself.

*What a bonus. James Warner, the son of the man who arrested me, verbally abused me, told me I was a freak and a disgusting animal is now under my control. Oh, this is going to be fun. I'll show that fucking cop animal!*

Looking back at Ashna, Gerard wondered how loud she'd scream. Should he wait until the businesses in the street closed before he started? Although he was reasonably confident the concrete walls were thick enough to contain most sounds, he knew a high-pitched scream could carry quite a distance under certain conditions. Gerard wasn't sure he wanted to take the chance. That's how they'd caught him last time—someone hearing.

Remembering the days he'd spent in prison tipped the scales towards caution. Gerard hated being caged up like an animal, hated being trapped and at the mercy of others.

*Yes, wait. It's the smart thing to do. Later they can make as much noise as they like. They can scream all weekend. In fact, I'm counting on it.*

Gerard had drifted off into a fantasy, imagining what he

would do, when the buzzer for the front door startled him.

*Who the fuck?*

After re-bolting the kitchen door, Gerard walked towards the front of the building, shutting the door between the warehouse and the office on his way through. When he looked through the Venetian blinds to see who was at the door, Gerard saw a man wearing a denim shirt embroidered with 'Wilson Rug Importers' across the top pocket. It was just a nosy neighbour.

Gerard turned the lock and opened the door. "Yes?"

"Hi, my name's Paul Wilson from the unit next-door. Just thought I'd pop over and welcome you to the neighbourhood."

"Pleased to meet you Paul," Gerard said extending his hand. "Look I'm a bit busy to talk at the moment, trying to sort myself out. You know what it's like when you first move into a new place."

"I just thought I'd let you know that if you need anything, pop next door, I'm always happy to help. I do good discounts for friends and neighbours too if you need any rugs."

"Thanks. I'll keep that in mind."

*Now fuck off.*

# CHAPTER 11 - FRIDAY AFTERNOON

Chris wracked his brain for answers. Warner had been right about the gate. The canine unit followed the scent left by James and Ashna across the schoolyard, but it vanished once they were through the gate and onto the street.

Canvassing the rest of the neighbourhood hadn't given them any more leads either. Everything they'd discovered so far had only confirmed their worst fears. The name on the van couldn't possibly be a coincidence, but without a license plate number, it looked unlikely they'd find it in a hurry. They didn't even know which direction it had gone. The whole episode had gone unnoticed. The ease with which Williamson had pulled of the abduction made Chris sick.

*How does someone take two kids from a school without anyone seeing a thing?*

He rubbed his temples, closing his eyes a moment, only to have the image of Leonard Bourne's bloody hand pop into his head. Blinking twice, Chris turned toward Andy who was leaning on their car studying his notes.

"Look mate, you and I know this area better than most right? I think the way to find Williamson is to hit the streets, meet all our contacts, and get the word out. We need to keep showing his photo around. This case is going to be a numbers game. The more people we talk to, and more places we visit, the better our odds of finding someone who's seen something."

"So where do you reckon we should start?"

Chris thought for a moment. "What say we try the cafés, restaurants, and supermarkets in the area first? Everybody's got to eat."

Andy nodded. "Then the motels and serviced apartments in Mount Victoria. He could be moving around but it's more likely he's found a bolthole somewhere. Never know, someone might remember him or the van."

After a short drive, their first stop was a small Mexican restaurant only five blocks from The Cloud Nine Club. Andy was keen to go there because of what he called 'the chilli factor'. Chris decided to humour him. Besides, he didn't have any better ideas.

They parked in front of the restaurant, made their way inside, and asked to speak to the manager. Twenty or so people were having lunch. The manager, a small man with a round cheery face greeted them. The large moustache that graced his upper lip reminded Andy of a Poncho Villa movie he'd once seen.

"Excuse us, but we need your assistance." Andy said showing the manager his identification. "Is there a private place we can talk?"

The manager nodded and led them to a small office. The office had a desk covered in paperwork, a chair, and filing cabinet. The office was tighter than an overstuffed burrito with all three of them in there.

"Now, what can I do to help?" The manager asked, his back pressed against the filing cabinet.

Chris placed a photo of Williamson on the desk. "Have you seen this man?"

"He doesn't look familiar. What's he done?"

"He's a suspect in relation to a kidnapping."

"Oh dear," the manager said, glancing once again at the photo.

"Would you mind getting your staff to have a look? Maybe one of them has seen him in the last couple of days," Chris asked.

"Sure, no problem. They're not all rostered on at the moment, but I'll tell those who are here to come in for a look."

Unfortunately, none of the staff recognized Williamson. One thought he looked vaguely familiar, but despite doing his best to remember, the waiter just couldn't be sure.

Chris left a copy of Williamson's photo, gave the manager his card, and asked him to show the photo to the other staff members.

"Ring me right away if someone has any information. It's important."

"Do you guys use the brand *Locos Jalapeños* here?" Andy asked in parting.

"Sure do," the manager replied. "They're the best. We buy

them by the case."

Andy filed the information away for future reference.

With one establishment down, and god knows how many to go, the two detectives realised they didn't have time to waste. They had to keep moving, and moving fast. Lives depended on it.

**********

At 2:00 p.m. Blondie rushed into Warner's office. "Hey boss, I think I've found the van. There's a guy in the Hutt Valley who sold one to a guy matching Williamson's description."

"Good stuff. Has he done an photo I.D. yet?"

"I've just emailed him the picture. I thought I'd ring him back from here and put him on speaker."

"Good idea, let's do it."

Warner crossed his fingers, and said a silent prayer as Blondie punched the number into the phone. When the receptionist answered, Blondie asked to be put through to the salesman. After three rings, a voice resonated through the speaker.

"Troy Simpson speaking, how can I help you?"

"Mr. Simpson, its Detective Green again, I've got Detective Inspector Robert Warner with me, you're on speaker phone. How did you go with the picture I sent? Did you recognize the guy?"

"I sure did. He bought a white Toyota Hi-Ace, 2.8, 5-speed manual. The one with the long wheelbase, it's a pretty popular model."

"Yes!" Blondie said pumping the air with her fist.

"When was this?" Warner asked.

"Tuesday, just after lunch if my memory is correct, let me see," the salesman said referring to his paperwork. "Yes here it is ... Tuesday."

"And there's no doubt it's the same guy?" Blondie asked.

"No doubt at all, his name is Tom Renfrew. I remember him quite clearly. He paid cash. I even helped him load his motorcycle into the van after completing the sale."

"Thanks, Mr Simpson, that's great." Warner said. "Look, I need you to email me any documentation you have right away. My assistant, Detective Green, will be there to take your statement in about half an hour."

"Okay," the salesman said. "I'll fire the details off to you now. Your assistant can ask for me at reception, they'll page me."

Warner disconnected the call. "Thank Christ, a break at last. Good work detective. You get going. Call me if anything important turns up. In the meantime, I'll grab his email as soon as it comes through, and get the plate number out to the troops."

Blondie stood up ready to go. "I wonder where he got the bike."

"Gerard never fails to surprise, that's for sure. Oh and see if they have security cameras on the lot, we might get the bike's rego number too."

Blondie raced down Harris Street as soon as the roller door was up far enough to get the car out. Now that they had a lead, the real work of hunting Williamson down could start. This was the reason she'd joined the police. Sure, she wanted to make a difference, but it was the thrill of the chase that really got her heart pumping.

Warner felt some small relief. Now, at least, they had a chance. When he heard the familiar bleep of an incoming email he opened the attachments and clicked print.

Taking the documents as they came off the printer, Warner started a list. Tom Renfrew was the alias. The address listed for Renfrew was the highest priority. Apartment 12, 334 Roseneath Terrace. Just up the hill from Oriental Bay. That was consistent with what their witness from the club had told them.

After making a quick call to a judge to obtain a search warrant, Warner spoke to despatch and got them to send the closest unmarked unit to keep an eye on Williamson's suspected address. "And tell them keep a low profile for Christ's sake, the idea is to follow him until we know where the kids are."

Warner knew that until they discovered the exact location of the two children, police couldn't risk apprehending Williamson. He had nothing to lose. If they arrested him too early, Gerard could deny all knowledge of the kidnapping, and James and Ashna could die before anyone found them. Police couldn't force Gerard to talk. New Zealand wasn't a country that looked favourably on torture or other unsavoury interrogation techniques. Still, if it came to the crunch, and if all else failed, Warner was prepared to beat the information out of Gerard. If it came down to losing his job or losing his son, the answer was a no brainer. He'd do whatever was necessary to get James back safely and face the consequences later.

Warner tried to think positively as he made arrangements for more squads to head up to Roseneath. Having this new information certainly upped the odds of getting the kids back safely. If Blondie was able to get the motorcycle's registration number from the car yard's security cameras that would be a bonus too. There was also the chance that when he ran the alias Tom Renfrew through police computer it might turn up other useful information, especially if Gerard had used the name before.

But the main lead so far was the address in Roseneath. If the address proved to be genuine, Warner would organise round-the-clock surveillance on the place. Gerard would surely turn up there eventually.

His hand shook slightly as he lifted the phone to call the Area Commander and request more manpower. Just as he started punching numbers, a knock sounded on his door and D.I. Watkins came into his office. Warner replaced the receiver.

"I'm sorry Robert, but the District Commander has just given me the lead on the Williamson and the Redford School case. You're going to have to bring me up to speed and step down."

Warner looked at Watkins, his face scrunched in disbelief. "Are you are fucking kidding me?"

**********

Chris and Andy had visited a number of establishments around the area, all to no avail. They decided to change tactics and took a side of the street each, showing Gerard's picture to all and sundry. Chris had just come out of a sushi shop, when Andy crossed the street, and came up to him.

"Hey Chris, just got a call from Warner, looks like they've found the yard that sold Williamson that van. Blondie's on her way there now. He's going by the name Tom Renfrew."

"Alright! Things are starting to happen."

"And they've got the address he used in the purchase. It's up on Roseneath Terrace. It looks like our dealer friend was right about him living up the hill. They're pretty sure the place is empty, but there's a unit keeping surveillance on it until the warrant arrives."

Chris would love to spend a private moment with Gerard if he got the chance. Maybe Gerard could conveniently resist arrest. Chris fantasized briefly about his fist meeting the bridge of Gerard's nose.

*Yes, that would be worth a few bruised knuckles.*

"Warner said the address could be bogus, but they should know soon enough."

"So, if it is his place, and it's empty. Where the fuck is he?" Chris asked.

"I've been thinking about that. We're not having much luck with the cafés and restaurants, so why don't we try some hardware stores? The assistant principal said the van was full of tools and equipment. He must have bought the stuff somewhere."

"But how's that going to help us?"

"Maybe someone in the shop struck up a conversation with him. You know all that salesmanship stuff … get to know your customer, make them feel at ease."

"Get them to buy things they don't need, with money they don't have more like," Chris added.

"Remember that little comment he made when he bought the speed? He might have let something slip. People talk too much for their own bloody good sometimes. Hey, it may not do any good, but unless you've got a better idea?"

Chris didn't have a better idea.

"Let's try Kaiwharawhara then," Chris suggested. "That's

where I'd go if I was looking for tools. There are two big places just down the road from each other."

After a ten-minute drive to the outskirts of town, the first hardware shop was coming up on the right. Andy indicated and pulled into the parking lot.

"You're dead right about people talking too much," Chris said. "If some of those cretins would just shut the fuck up, they wouldn't end up in jail. They always think they're so bloody clever and add lots of detail rather than keeping it simple. The bullshit starts flowing, and they put their foot in it. "

"Yeah, remember that plonker who told us he didn't even like blonde chicks when we questioned him on that rape case last year?"

"Yep, how'd he know the girl was blonde? Moron. At least the idiots make our job easier."

Andy stopped near the entrance and the two detectives got out of the car. The store was a huge barn of a place and had everything anyone could possibly need when building or renovating.

Once through the automatic doors, Chris flashed his I.D. at the first staff member he saw. "My name is Detective Spacey. Is the manager here?"

"Hang on a minute, I'll get him." The woman at the checkout picked up her phone.

Only a minute had passed before a middle-aged man wearing the company's livery arrived beside them. "Hi, I'm Tane Hawera, the manager. What can I do for you?"

Chris opened his folio and showed him Gerard's picture. "We need to find out if you or any of your staff have served this guy in the last couple of days? We think he may have been shopping in this area."

"Maybe ..."

"What do you mean maybe?" Chris and Andy said in unison.

"Well he looks sort of familiar, but I'm not a hundred percent sure. I might have seen him in the shop. We get a lot of people through here you know."

"I'm sure you do. Would you mind asking your staff to have a look Mr. Hawera? Maybe one of them will remember him." Chris said.

"Sure, give me a few minutes. I'll do the rounds and get the staff to come and see you. Why don't you wait in my office, just through there," the manager said, pointing towards a door on their left.

"Thanks, and could you do it quickly? We need this info yesterday."

The manager wasted no time in speaking to each of his staff members as he walked briskly around the shop.

"Yeah, I remember the guy," the sixth person to view the photo said. "I sold him a whole bunch of stuff a couple of days ago."

"Did he say much?" Andy asked.

"A little ... he seemed to know what he was looking for. Didn't muck around."

"Think hard and tell us anything you can remember." Andy urged the young man.

"Let me think. Um . . . I do remember asking him what sort of building project he was doing. He said he was a sculptor ... was doing up his studio."

"His studio?" Chris asked.

"Yeah, I'm pretty sure that's what it was. You know, I talk to so many people each day it's hard keeping them straight sometimes."

Chris nodded. "Fair enough, but you're reasonably sure he said sculptor and studio?"

The sales assistant looked up and to the left, eyes slightly closed. "Yeah, I wouldn't stake my life on it, but I've got a good memory. I'm pretty sure it was him that said studio."

"Anything else you can think of?"

"I remember he paid cash," the salesman said. "We get a little bonus for cash sales over $500."

"Okay ...um...Danny," Chris said, reading from the name-tag on the salesman's shirt. "I don't suppose you could find us a copy of the sales receipt?"

"Hang on, I'll look it up and make a copy for you."

Danny left the office and returned a few minutes later with a sheet of A4 paper with a photocopy of the sales receipt on it. "Here you go, hope it helps."

"It all helps," Andy said taking the receipt.

Chris turned to the manager. "We'll leave this photo with you. Here's my card, ring me right away if he shows up again."

"I will," the manager promised.

As they left the shop, Andy's eyes were scanning the invoice. "Just a lot of general building stuff here, some tools, a slide bolt, a couple of padlocks. We already know what he did with one of those. It certainly looks like our guy's up to something. Why else would he need more than one padlock?"

"So he's rented space somewhere, and has James and Ashna stashed there." Chris said as the two detectives approached their car.

"That would be the logical conclusion."

"So how do we find it?"

"Let's concentrate on the real estate agents. If he's rented a studio space it shouldn't take that long to find it surely."

"Right, how many can there be?" Chris nodded.

"Back to the station so we can hit the phones I reckon."

"Sounds like a plan Sherlock. Seeing we're in a hurry I'd better drive." Chris liked any excuse to drive fast, and as excuses went, this was a good one. He always accused Andy of driving like his grandmother, only slower.

There was a squeal of rubber as Chris stomped on the accelerator, fishtailing out of the parking lot. Andy hit the switch for the lights and siren, and braced himself for the ride.

**********

Within twenty minutes, there were six plain-clothed officers, stationed near the apartment on Roseneath Terrace. There was no sign of a white van. Police stationed at each end of the street were ready to alert the others if Gerard came back. Two specialists were ready to enter the apartment as soon as the warrant arrived, and there were two unmarked cars around the corner ready to follow Gerard if and when he showed up.

Police knew the apartment was empty. A thermal imaging device hadn't detected any body heat coming from its interior. The entry team would do a quick search, hide a couple of small transmitters, and then get out again before Williamson arrived back as soon as the warrant turned up. If Williamson returned without the two children, the most likely scenario in Warner's opinion, they'd put a tracking device on his van as well, providing they could do so without alerting him to their presence.

"Entry team, get ready to move," the Detective Sergeant in charge of the operation said into his microphone. "The warrant's not far away."

An unmarked car had collected the paperwork from the judge, and was rushing it back to Roseneath. A few minutes later, the car pulled up just around the corner from 334. The driver handed the warrant to the Sergeant who quickly scanned the document to make sure the details were correct.

"Entry team clear to go, we have authority. I repeat we are clear to go."

"Copy, moving now."

The two officers wasted no time. They had the door to Williamson's apartment open in seconds, and began searching the place from top to bottom. Even though there wasn't a hell of a lot to search, they still had to work fast.

One of the officers got a mild shock when he opened a dresser drawer and discovered a large pile of banknotes. It looked like a year's salary just sitting there. There was also a passport in the name of Thomas Renfrew lying in the drawer beside the cash. The picture in the passport was, without any doubt, Gerard Williamson.

The officer pushed the button on his radio. "I've found a passport confirming this is Williamson's place."

"Copy," the Sergeant replied. "Keep moving. I want you out of there pronto."

Photographing the details of the passport, and doing a quick estimate of the cash, the officer moved on looking for anything that might give an indication of where Gerard might be holding the kids.

Their chances of nabbing the bastard had just gone up. The discovery of the false passport was an added bonus. Williamson wouldn't be leaving the country using that alias anytime soon. Unfortunately, the rest of the apartment yielded nothing.

After the quick search, officers placed the bugs. The first one went on the underside of the kitchen table, the second into the light fitting in the bathroom. They were small, transmitting sound only, but that was all that was required. The last one went into the phone receiver, not that it would be of much use in this case. The phone wasn't connected.

Once the bugs were in place, the officers went to the garage and opened up the storage locker assigned to Gerard's apartment. The only things in it were the bike, a helmet, and a pair of gloves. They made a note of the bikes rego, attached a tracking device, and left the scene, mission accomplished.

Police would now keep the apartment under surveillance, and hope for Gerard's return.

**********

While Gerard waited for the other businesses in the area to close, he had a bit of time to kill. The rug guy next door had given him a fright. He lit a cigarette and looked at his watch. It would only be an hour or so until the street was deserted. This would be the weekend of his life. A shiver ran down his spine as he fantasized about all the fun he was going to have. He'd just check on the children again, and then treat himself to another line of speed.

When Gerard opened the door to the kitchen area, James and Ashna were still sitting on the floor where he'd left them, backs to the wall, huddled together. The girl had her head down on the boy's shoulder, one arm thrown across her face. The boy looked up and glared at Gerard with a look of utter contempt.

He was a tough little guy, no doubt about it. Tough nuts were always the tastiest to crack, but crack he would, like a walnut at

Christmas. Gerard glared back at James.

*My game, my rules you little brat.*

It took a minute or so of intense staring, but the boy finally looked away. Gerard smiled in satisfaction.

*That's right, I'm the boss.*

Locking the door, Gerard went into the office and grabbed a small packet of speed out of his jacket pocket. He pulled the cord, closing the blinds fully, before spilling a small amount of powder from the envelope onto the Formica counter. Using a plastic card from his wallet, he chopped the tiny pile into fine dust, carefully creating two lines. Then, using a rolled up 20-dollar bill, he snorted a line up each nostril.

**********

"Okay, now that he's gone again," James whispered.

"What are you going to do?"

"Well, when I was looking through the cupboards, I saw bricks around the drainpipe where it goes through the back wall. The mortar's crumbling, so I thought I'd try to get the pipe undone and loosen the bricks. Once they're out, we might be able to squeeze through."

"But what if he catches you?"

"We've got to try something Ashna."

"But … but you said the police would find us soon."

"They probably will, but I want to try, just in case. Can you listen and tell me if you hear him coming back while I have a look?"

"Okay James, but be quiet."

James went to the sink and opened the cupboard door. He looked closely at the area where the pipe went through the concrete wall. It was rectangular in shape, three bricks wide and four bricks high. He figure there must have been a vent or something running through the wall at some time. Around the pipe was a gap where the square bricks didn't quite meet the round pipe. Whoever had done the job had stuffed strips of rag covered in mortar into the gaps rather than cut bricks to shape.

The patch didn't look all that strong.

James started tugging at the material around the pipe. It was old and rotten. A few small clumps came away in his hand. Taking the scissors from his pocket, he dug out more of the packing. After a few minutes, he'd created a hole big enough to squeeze his hand through. Peering through the hole, he could see a clay bank about two feet away, and smell the rotting leaves and other debris that had fallen down between the bank and the wall.

If he got all the packing out, disconnected the drainpipe, and removed the bricks, the hole might be big enough for them to crawl through, just.

**********

Robert Warner was still fuming. Detective Inspector Watkins, under orders from the District Commander, had relieved him of authority in the Williamson case. He'd spent the last half hour or so bringing Watkins up to speed with everything he knew.

"I can't see why I can't stay working on this. Nobody knows Gerard like I do," Warner complained. "Finding the van proves that."

"People can't remain objective when they've got a personal interest in a case, and you know it." Watkins replied. "Surely you must realise this is for the best."

"So I'm supposed to sit here and do nothing? He's my son for Christ's sake!"

"Look Robert you've done a good job so far. The apartment's under surveillance. His bike has a tracking device on it. We have extra teams searching for him all over town. His vehicle registration numbers are on the hot list. Just leave it to me. Okay? You're not the only competent person in the Wellington Police you know. We'll find him."

"But surely I can do something."

"I'm sorry mate, but you know the rules. Look, I know how helpless you feel but please, let me do my job. Okay? The District Commander told me that if I didn't get your full cooperation, or if he discovers you're interfering in any way whatsoever, you'll be suspended. Why don't you go home and look after your wife?"

Even though Warner could see the sense in the arguments put before him, he wasn't about to stop trying to find his son.

*Fuck the rules.*

"I hear you, but that doesn't mean I like it," Warner said. "Just keep me informed. Okay? Don't treat me like a civilian."

"Don't worry. I'll let you know if anything happens." Watkins replied. "You keep your nose out of it, and I'll keep you up to date. Deal?"

"Okay, deal." Warner lied.

Satisfied, Watkins picked up the stack of files and marched out the door. Warner's stare burned a hole into his back as he left. As soon as the door closed, Warner picked up the phone and started to dial.

"Is that you Chris?" Warner asked.

"No it's Andy here. Chris just stepped out a moment. Is that you Detective Inspector?"

"Yeah, I'm just ringing to tell you the address Williamson gave the car yard is real. Found a bike of his too. What about you guys, any luck?"

"We've been showing Williamson's picture around and got a lead from a shop we visited."

"What sort of lead?" Warner said all ears now.

"Well, it's nothing solid, but it seems Williamson bought some stuff at a hardware store a couple of days ago. He made an offhand comment to the salesman … said he was doing up a studio. Don't know if it's anything or not, but we thought we'd check out the real estate agencies … see if someone matching Williamson's description has leased premises recently. We're hitting the phones."

"Good work. Were you planning on telling anyone about this?"

Andy swallowed. "Not yet, um … we thought we'd explore the possibilities ourselves a little first."

Andy, expecting a reprimand, heard Warner clear his throat instead.

"Hey, can I ask for your help with something Andy?"

"Shoot."

"The District Commander has taken me off the case. He says I can't be objective because my son James is one of the children that have been abducted. It's D.I. Watkins' baby now."

"You obviously disagree."

"I understand where he's coming from, but fuck Watkins and the District Commander if they think I'm going to sit around with my finger up my arse when my son is missing. Problem is you see … I can't let them know that. You hear me?"

"Yeah, I hear you. So what do you want from us?"

"I was hoping you'd keep me in the loop. I don't trust Watkins. Besides, if you guys find that psycho I'd like to be in on the arrest. I want some private time with that arsehole."

"I see," Andy said, hesitating slightly. "Let me run this past Chris. I'll see what I can do. Okay?"

"Sure Andy. Thanks."

As Andy hung up the phone, Chris walked into their office with an extra set of phone books.

"I just got a call from Warner. He's fuming because he's been bumped off the case, it being his kid and all. D.I. Watkins is in charge now."

"What else did Warner say?"

"Wants us to keep him informed, and let him help with an arrest if we find out where Williamson is. I think 'fuck Watkins and the District Commander,' were his exact words. Says he wants some private time with Williamson."

"I hope you told him to take a number and go to the back of the queue." Chris said. "Still, I can understand where he's coming from. I'd want in too if it was my kid."

"Look we're already pushing the envelope. If the brass find out we aren't going through proper channels we'll be back in uniform faster than you can say the words disciplinary hearing."

"But haven't we already bent the rules doing that deal with the drug dealer? Now here we are looking for a studio."

Andy looked hard at Chris. "Yeah okay, we're a little out of order. But even if by some stroke of luck we stumble across

Williamson how could we possibly bring Warner in? "

"I hear you. It's way too risky to involve Warner. But," Chris said raising his eyebrows, "if we can cover our arses and get him ourselves ..."

"Cover our arses is right pal, fucked if I want to end up out in the middle of nowhere writing traffic tickets."

"Hey, stop worrying. We've got to find the crazy bastard first."

**********

As Warner sat at his desk reflecting on his conversation with Andy, Blondie returned from interviewing the car salesman.

"The security cams didn't get the number plate for Williamson's bike." Blondie said as she dropped a copy of her notes on Warner's desk.

"That's okay. The team that searched Williamson's apartment found the bike in his storage locker."

"That's good news. So, it's stakeout time I take it."

"You got it. With luck Williamson will lead us back to where he's got Ashna and James stashed. The bad news is I'm off the case. Watkins is in charge now, conflict of interest according to the DC."

"Just like that?"

"Yup, just like that. Watkins said I'd be up shit creek if I so much as fart in Williamson's direction. He wants a word with you by the way. Probably wants you to stay onboard."

"You sound annoyed."

"Well wouldn't you be? The truth is, I don't give a damn what they say. I'm not going to sit around while that fruit loop has my boy."

"So what's the plan boss?"

"I rang Andy. Told him I wanted to be kept in the loop."

"What'd he say?"

"Said he'd do what he could. He also mentioned a lead they'd picked at a hardware store they visited. It seems Williamson mention to one of the staff he was doing up a studio."

"Well that's a start. They working it themselves or just passing the info on to Watkins?"

"Working it ... for the moment anyway. I also told them I want in on the arrest if they find him." As soon as Warner spoke the words he realised now how silly he must sound.

The look on Blondie's face and the shake of her head confirmed it. "You know as well as I do that that's asking for trouble. Everyone would end up on report."

"I know but...."

"Hey look, I'll keep my ear to the ground and keep you informed. I promise. I'll also talk to Chris and persuade him to keep you posted. You know that's about the best you can hope for at the moment eh?"

"Yeah I know. It's just...."

"Don't worry Boss we'll find them."

"And you don't mind talking to Chris?"

"No I don't mind," Blondie replied, suppressing a smile.

"Thanks. In the meantime, I'm going to start phoning a few real estate agents and try to find this studio the boys think he's rented. Could you let Chris know I'm going to use his name in my enquiries ... you know ... to keep under the radar?"

"Just don't drop him in it," Blondie said. "I'd better let him know what you're up to so he can cover your arse if need be. I'll ring you once I've spoken to him. Just don't go off half-cocked. Okay? I don't need the hassle of having to train up a new boss on top of everything else that's going on right now."

Warner forced a grin onto his face. "Don't worry about me. I'm not going to do anything silly. Now go and see Watkins." Warner waved her away. "Let me get onto this. I only have an hour or so before everyone will be gone for the night. And for Christ's sake don't forget to tell me if you hear anything."

"Relax," Blondie said as she walked towards the door. "I'll phone you once I've spoken to Watkins."

But before she went to see D. I. Watkins, Blondie thought she might find a nice quiet place and give Chris a ring. Hopefully she could arrange to see him later.

She laughed at herself. This man was making her feel like a

teenager again.

**********

James had managed to remove all of the packing from around the drainpipe. Looking at the mess he'd made in the bottom of the cupboard, he wondered what he should do with it. Whatever it was, he'd better do it fast. He checked his watch. It was 4:40 p.m. He'd been at it for over half an hour. Sure, he could shut the cupboard door, but if the man opened it for any reason, it would blow their escape plan. Rubbing his bruised jaw, he considered his options.

Ashna had her ear pressed against the door. "Still quiet James, how much longer?"

"I've got all the packing out, now I've just got to get rid of it."

"Well hurry, he could come back at any time."

James took a handful of shredded material, eased his hand past the pipe, and dropped the scrap on the other side of the wall. After repeating this procedure a couple of times, he swept the last of the crumbs into a small pile, scooped them up into his palm, and deposited them with the others.

Next, James started working on the drainpipe itself. Fortunately, it was plastic, and made from sections held together with joiners. The pipe had a U-bend, then a 90-degree junction that turned the pipe towards the wall. Another junction on the far side of the wall took the pipe between the building and the bank towards the sewer trap. He could reach the U-bend easily, but the other junctions could be tricky.

Twisting the top collar that held the U-bend in place, James was pleased to discover he could turn it without much difficulty. He loosened it just a little, not wanting it to leak, and then tried the joint at the bottom. This junction was a bit stiff, barely moving with his first attempt. Not being one to give up, James wiped his damp hands on his shirt and tried again. This time the collar moved a bit more. A few more attempts and it started to free up.

The next junction was the hardest to get loose. There was very little room for James to manoeuvre his hand around the pipe and through the wall. Lying on his back, jammed under the shelf, with his hands through the wall James finally got the junction loose. With this task completed James began to feel more confident his plan would work.

Now the whole section of pipe should only take a minute or two for him to disassemble when the time came. He got up and ran the tap, rinsed off his hands and dried them on the towel hanging above the sink. Checking to make sure that he hadn't loosened any of the pipes so much as to cause a leak, he turned off the tap and went to sit beside Ashna for a rest.

"I've loosened all the pipes," James said. "I'm not positive, but I think we'll be able to squeeze through the hole once I've knocked the bricks out."

"What do we do if we can't fit through?"

"I'm not sure. Have you got any ideas?"

**********

Since they'd been back at the station, Chris and Andy had each phoned six or seven real estate firms. It was slow and tedious work. For all their efforts thus far, they'd both come up with a big fat zero.

It took far longer to complete each call than Chris had expected. By the time he'd dialled the number, talked to the receptionist, got put on hold, was forced to listen to some canned crap masquerading as music, got transferred to a different person, repeated the story, got put on hold again while yet another person was tracked down, then explained the story for a third time, described Williamson and asked whether or not their company had leased anything in the last couple of days to a person fitting his description, ten minutes or more would have passed.

Then, after all the thumb-twiddling and foot-tapping, he'd be told that nothing fitting that description had been leased in the last few days, but they could check further back into their records, if he didn't mind holding."

Chris groaned. "Jesus, this is going to take forever. There must be a quicker way."

Being on hold was the worst. After five minutes of muzak Chris was ready to kill the inventor of the phone system if only he knew where they lived.

As Chris dialled another number prepared to yell 'don't you dare put me on hold', he looked at Andy and frowned. "We've only got another 45 minutes before everyone will have gone home for the weekend, then what are we going to do?"

Andy pondered Chris's question.

"If you wanted to find a place to rent, you'd look online, or in the newspaper right?" It wasn't really a question, Andy was just thinking aloud. "So maybe we should do the same. I somehow doubt Gerard has an internet connection so let's find some recent newspapers and phone the firms advertising the sort of places he might go for."

"Now you're thinking." Chris said hanging up and rising from his chair. "The papers for the last few days should still be in the staff room. I'll go have a look."

Chris didn't waste any time making his way down the hallway. The staff room was a mess. There were empty food containers left on the table, and the sink was full of dirty dishes. Coffee cups, newspapers and magazines littered every available surface. Wondering if the cleaners were on strike again, Chris quickly collected whatever newspapers he could find, and headed back to their office.

"Fuck you should see the mess in there man, dishes and crap everywhere." Chris threw a pile of newspapers onto the desk. "Here's everything I could find. Watch out there's something that smells pretty rank on some of these."

"Yuck!" Andy said, holding one section up between two fingers before dropping the lot carefully into the bin. "Let's just toss everything that isn't classifieds into the bin, then we'll date order the rest and get to work. Okay?"

"Aye aye sir!" Chris said, snapping his hand to his forehead in mock salute.

It didn't take the detectives long to sift though the material they had. Then it was a matter of scanning the 'to lease' column as quickly as possible and listing any that looked promising.

There were quite a few ads in each newspaper, but many they discounted straight away. Anything over five thousand square feet was too large and possibly too expensive. They also figured that buildings on a main road were unlikely candidates. Gerard would want something discreet, away from the public eye.

"Time is of the essence mate," Andy said in a rush of words. "Let's just give ourselves 15 minutes to list the ones that look the most promising and then hit the phones again."

"Why don't you do the scanning and I'll start phoning right away. We might get lucky."

"Works for me."

**********

Gerard wasn't hungry, but he knew he should try to eat something to maintain his energy levels. It was nearly 5:00 p.m. and he'd been rushing around all day. Food had been the last thing on his mind. He was getting impatient at having to wait for playtime. Rather than walking around in circles until the street was deserted, he decided to drive the few kilometres into Lower Hutt and grab some takeaways. He couldn't face baked beans or something out of a tin. Fish and chips or a burger would hit the spot and give him the strength he'd need for the evening ahead. The two kids certainly weren't going anywhere.

Unlocking the door, Gerard poked his head into the back room to check on James and Ashna one last time before he left. Both were sitting in much the same position as the last time he'd seen them. James looked up as he entered. Ashna averted her eyes.

*Such a shy wee thing, she's going to be such fun.*

"You brats hungry?" Gerard asked, looking at James while raising his eyebrows. "If you are, tell me what you want. Burgers or fish and chips?"

James leaned down and spoke softly to Ashna. "You hungry Ashna, we should try to eat."

"Make your bloody minds up, I don't have all day." Gerard said.

"Fish and chips," said James, making a decision for the two of them.

"Please!"

"Fish and chips … please," James repeated begrudgingly.

"Now you two keep quiet. If I hear a peep out of you, you'll regret it."

Gerard closed the door and slid the bolt back into position.

As soon as the door closed, James leaped to his feet and pressed his ear against the door. He heard the van start, and what he thought was the roller door opening.

"Right, I'm going to start scraping the mortar Ashna, you listen out for him coming back. Okay?"

"Okay," Ashna said, a bit of steadiness coming back into her voice.

James opened the cupboard door and grabbed one of the teaspoons. Holding the spoon by the rounded end, he scraped at the gaps between the bricks until one arm got tired, then switched hands and scraped some more. After ten minutes or so of hard work, he'd managed to loosen a palm full of material. His hands were sore where the spoon had jabbed into his palms, and a series of red indentations had developed on each palm.

"How's it going James?" Ashna whispered.

"Slowly, my hands are getting sore. I need something to wrap around them," James said.

Then he remembered the first aid kit. He took one of the crepe bandages from the kit, and wrapped it around his right palm. Picking up the spoon again, he gave it a test.

"This will work I think," James said as much to himself as to Ashna before attacking the mortar with every ounce of strength he had. Every few minutes he'd take a short break, rest his arm, and wipe the sweat out of his eyes before starting again. When he had a handful of material, he'd deposit it on the other side of the wall out of sight. After 15 minutes hard slog, James managed to loosen one of the bricks which split in half as he'd pulled it out. He put it with the other rubble near the clay bank.

"That spoon's getting pretty munted," James said to Ashna, "But if I have enough time, I reckon I can loosen all the bricks."

Ashna had been thinking as she sat with her ear pressed up against the door. Her initial shock was starting to wear off, and she was returning to her normal analytical self. She'd come up with a possible escape plan too, and had nearly convinced herself it would work. If the man decided to do something to them soon, it might be their only chance.

If this was the man she'd overheard her brothers talking about, she didn't want to wait a moment longer than necessary.

**********

Chris and Andy were at their desks with phones in their hands and newspapers scattered about the floor of their office.

"I don't care who I speak to," Chris was saying into the phone. "I just need this info as soon as poss. Two lives depend on it. Don't put me on ho...."

"One moment sir," the receptionist said over the top of him before he had a chance to finish. Then the dreadful music started.

"Shit!" Chris said in frustration. "The fuckers put me on hold again."

"Right, here's the last of the list. I'll start at the bottom and work up."

They both knew the chances of finding Gerard's studio today, assuming he'd even leased one, were running out. By 5:30 p.m. the offices would close, and the employees would head off.

The agent picked up the phone. "Clarkson here, how can I help?"

"My name's Detective Spacey, Wellington Police. Please don't put me on hold. I was wondering if you've leased that 145 square meter warehouse unit in Johnsonville yet. I'm trying to track down a felon who's been looking for space in your area."

"Why yes, I think one of our agents signed it up yesterday, Please hold."

Click went the phone.

"Fuck!" Chris shouted down the receiver. "What's wrong with

you? Are you fucking deaf?"

He looked up at the clock on the wall. Time seemed to be passing much faster than normal. It was already 5:25 p.m. This was likely to be his last call before business phones were diverted to answering machines, and his chances of finding the studio today evaporated.

5 minutes later Clarkson was back.

"Detective, I'm sorry to keep you waiting. Look, I've just spoken to the agent concerned. An electrical contracting company leased the unit yesterday. The agent assures me he knows the principal personally, doesn't look like it's the one you're after."

"Okay, thanks for your help." Chris hung the phone up. A sigh escaped his lips as he scratched one more off the list. "Damn!"

When Chris looked up, Andy had his phone glued to his ear and was talking urgently into the mouthpiece.

Chris tried the next number on the list. "You have reached the office of Southern Real…"

Chris put a question mark next to the number and dialled the next. "Thank you for calling Hutt…"

When an answer phone started for a third time, Chris slammed down the phone. "Shit. They're all gone for the weekend."

Deciding he needed coffee, Chris got up and walked into Andy's field of vision. He mimed a drinking motion, and saw Andy nod in agreement.

When he returned to their office a few minutes later with two steaming cups, Andy was writing furiously on the pad in front of him. Putting a cup down in front of his colleague, Chris took a seat and listened to Andy's conversation.

"Yes." Andy mumbled as he wrote. "Right … and this was when? Okay. Is it possible for me to email you the picture of the guy we're looking for? Okay, great. Can you please tell the agent we need this identification done now, and not to leave until he's had a chance to look at it? There are two lives at stake here. Thanks. Yes … yes, I've got the address."

"A possibility?" Chris said lifting his eyebrows.

"Yep, I'm going to fire an email off to him now. I'll ring him back in a few minutes and see if we're in luck."

Andy typed the briefest of cover notes, attached the photo of Williamson and hit send.

"Don't forget your coffee. It might be a long day," Chris said, before taking a drink from his own cup.

Andy had a few quick slurps, and then looked up at the clock. Deciding enough time had passed since sending the email, he picked up the phone and hit the redial button.

Chris was just about to try one more agency when his cell phone rang.

"Hi Blondie," Chris said. "Yeah we've found one possibility. Andy's just emailed a picture off to them. He's in the process of phoning them back now."

"Fingers crossed eh?" Blondie said. "Hey you want to meet up later?"

"Yeah I'd like that. Hang on a tick, Andy's just hanging up."

When Chris looked at Andy's face, he knew straight away that they hadn't found Williamson. The shake of Andy's head confirmed Chris's suspicion.

"No, not him Blondie. We're still in the dark down here. Look, why don't we meet at the Southern Cross again?"

"How does eight sound?"

"Perfect. Just ring me if you get held up."

"Will do … oh by the way, Warner's following your lead and ringing a few rental agencies. Hope you don't mind but he thought he'd use your name so he could stay under the radar."

"Okay, as long as he doesn't do anything stupid."

"Nah, he said he'd play it cool. Well … I'll catch you later."

"You will indeed." Chris smiled as he put his cell phone back into his pocket. Then he turned to Andy. "So partner, any ideas?"

"Not off the top of my head. You?"

"Not really. Blondie said Warner's been phoning real estate agents too. I'm meeting her later to talk about it."

"Hey just a thought, we could still visit the addresses given in the adverts. Check them out and see if there's any activity inside.

What do you think? If Williamson isn't at his apartment, he must be somewhere else. I'm not meeting Blondie till eight, so that'll give us a couple of hours."

"That's fine with me. I've got nothing better to do. Let's hit the road. What area should we concentrate on do you think?" Andy asked.

"What area has the most possibilities? We may as well check out as many as we can, in what time we've got."

"Let me see here," Andy said scrolling through the list. "There are two in Petone, and another three in Lower Hutt that are all reasonably close to each other. We could get around those in a couple of hours if we hurry. The rest are all over the show."

"Right, Let's do it."

"I'll ring Warner and let him know what we're up to," Andy said. "You grab the car, and I'll meet you out front in a tick."

"Sounds like a plan."

**********

Gerard drove up the main street in Lower Hutt looking for the fish and chip shop he'd seen the other day on the way to the real estate agent's office. Peering at the shop fronts as he drove along, he finally spotted an illuminated sign advertising 'Chinese Meals, Fish & Chips'. Pulling into a parking space, he locked the van and walked briskly into the shop and up to the counter. The place was half-full of customers waiting for their Friday night treat.

A young woman behind the counter stood ready to take his order, her pen poised above a small pad. The white apron tied around her waist had seen better days, but was immaculately clean. She looked at Gerard expectantly.

"Four pieces of fish and two scoops of chips," He said.

She made a quick note on the paper, and tallied the order in record speed.

"Fourteen dollars eighty," the woman said holding her hand out for payment.

Gerard dropped a slightly curled twenty-dollar bill into her palm, took his change, and settled down on a plastic chair beside the counter. He tapped his foot impatiently as he waited. The speed, and excitement of what was to come, was jangling his nerves.

Grabbing a woman's magazine from a low table beside his chair, Gerard had a quick flip through its pages before abandoning it for a fishing magazine.

In just under 10 minutes his order was called and a parcel wrapped in white paper placed on the countertop. He grabbed the bundle and poked a hole in one end of the paper to let the steam out as he headed back to the van. Gerard hated soggy chips. Then waiting for a gap in the traffic, he did a U-turn, and drove back towards the workshop, keen to get back to the warehouse.

**********

James, aware of how much time that had passed, and that the man could come back any time, removed the bandage from around his hand and stuffed it into his pocket. Checking to see that he'd swept all the incriminating evidence away, he closed the cupboard door before sitting back down beside Ashna.

**********

Robert Warner decided to call real estate agents on the northern outskirts of Wellington. His logic being, rentals in those suburbs were cheaper, and a little more isolated. The suburbs would suit someone like Gerard who needed to keep out of the public eye. Unfortunately, the last two he'd rung had gone for the day.

As Warner tried to figure out his next move, his phone rang.

"Warner."

"Any news of James?" Julia asked.

Warner could tell she'd been crying. His wife sounded like she had a head cold. It was important that he stay strong for her.

He was pleased Julia's sister was with her. He felt guilty not being there himself, but sitting with Julia wasn't going to find their boy. Here at least, he might be of some use.

"Nothing so far sweetheart, but we're doing absolutely everything possible. Don't worry we'll find him." Warner smacked himself lightly on the forehead.

*Duh … how could she not worry?*

"Look sweetheart, as much as I'd like to be there with you, I need to stay here if I'm going to be of any use in finding James. You understand that don't you?"

It would drive Warner bonkers at home, pacing the house like a caged tiger.

"I understand Robert, just find our boy."

"I will, I promise. Look I'd better go. I'll see you soon sweetheart."

Warner hung up the phone, then reached down and opened up his bottom desk drawer eyeing the bottle lying on its side. He reached down to grab it, but then shook his head and closed the drawer again.

Warner leaned back in his chair exhausted and stared at the opposite wall.

*Just wait until I get my hands on you Gerard!*

The walls felt like they were closing in on him, the gloom of evening increasing. He couldn't think of what to do next. Helplessness was not a familiar feeling, and it was driving him to despair.

Blondie bustling into his office, snapped him out of his trance.

"I'm meeting Detective Spacey at eight so I'll ring you if any new leads turn up. He's okay about you using his name."

"Hey, thanks for that," Warner said. "I'm going to hang in a bit longer, keep my eye on things here. Watkins said he'd call later, so I'll wait for that before I head off home."

"How's Julia doing?"

"She's coping … just. There must be some way I can help find Williamson, but I can't seem to think straight at the moment."

"Just hang in there boss. We're doing everything we can."

Blondie had just left his office when Andy called informing him of their plan to check a few places Gerard might have rented in the Petone and Lower Hutt area.

"Thanks for the update. I appreciate it. Call me if you find anything."

After sitting with his head in his hands for a while, Warner stood up and walked over to a locked cupboard on the far side of his office. Inside the cupboard was a place to hang clothes and three drawers. In one of the locked drawers was a small calibre pistol, in another a box of ammunition. After loading the pistol, Warner slipped it into a specially constructed pocket on the inside of his jacket. Then he sat down at his desk again, opened the drawer, and reached for the bottle.

**********

Chris and Andy were driving towards a small warehouse unit they'd seen advertised in Cornish Street. It seemed the sort of place Gerard would like, and it was the nearest on their list. Rush hour was in full flow, so the Hutt Motorway was congested. Two lanes of bumper-to-bumper traffic were snaking around the harbour, heading home after the working week. They decided to run with their siren and lights as far as they could, trying to make the most of what little time they had.

Killing the siren, they turned left into Cornish Street and cruised down the street looking for the number.

"There it is," Andy said, pointing to a white building on their left."

"Park a bit further on, we can walk back. If Williamson's here we don't want him to see us."

They parked behind a shipping container sitting in front of a tile shop at the end of the street and crept back towards the white building.

Andy put his hand on his forehead to shield his eyes and pressed his nose against the window as he tried to peer past the security grill into the office. "Nothing in the office except an old counter. The place looks empty. Can't see inside the workshop."

"There's still a 'For Lease' sign on the wall up there. Let's see if we can see anything through the roller door. There might be a gap we can get a squiz through."

Inspecting the door, Chris spotted a rust hole, the size of a small coin, three feet above eye level. He gave Andy a boost up so he could see through the hole.

"Can you see anything?" Chris said straining under Andy's weight.

"I can see a few empty cartons, a bit of scrap timber and an old crate, but nothing else. The place looks deserted, definitely no van. No one moving around and I can't hear any noise."

"Let's check with the neighbours, they may have seen something," Chris suggested, lowering Andy back to the ground.

Walking to the unit next door, they saw the sign in the window stating the rug importers office hours, 8:30 a.m. to 5:30 p.m. Monday to Friday.

Andy checked his watch. "It's five past six this guy's gone for the weekend."

"Bugger."

"Yeah, and the tile shop is closed too." Andy looked up and down the street. "This place is like a ghost town."

"This doesn't look like it. Let's get going and try the next one."

**********

Gerard arrived back at the unit at 6:10. He'd heard a siren a few blocks away as he drove back to the unit, but it was a street or two over, and heading fast in the opposite direction.

As the roller door rose, Gerard pulled the van inside. The only activity he'd noticed in the street was an elderly couple getting ready to walk a pair of standard poodles. They'd just parked at the end of the street, and by the looks of it, were taking the dogs for a walk up the gully. No one else was about.

*Perfect. As soon as those dog walkers come back, I can start.*

"Food time." Gerard said to himself. The smell of fish and chips was making his stomach rumble. Grabbing the parcel from the passenger seat, he made his way towards the back room.

When Gerard opened the door, James and Ashna were sitting in exactly the same position they'd been in when he's left them thirty minutes ago. Gerard walked towards the cupboard.

James felt Ashna tense up. Bending down, the man opened the right-hand door, and reached for something on the shelf. The kids held their breath.

Gerard grabbed a jar of *Locos Jalapeños*, closed the door and sat down on the floor near James and Ashna.

Gerard opened the parcel, and put the jar of chillies on one corner of the paper. The four battered pieces of terakihi, and big pile of chips looked crisp and tasty.

"Come on you two, dig in," Gerard said.

*You'll need your strength for tonight.*

James nudged Ashna, encouraging her to eat something. He wasted no time himself, moving closer to the food, and grabbing a piece of fish.

"Come on Ashna, eat some food. You must be starving. I know I am," James said.

Ashna was afraid of the stranger, but eventually her hunger overcame her fear.

They ate in silence. Ashna looked at the food, keeping her eyes down the whole time, while James looked up between bites to glare at the man. Gerard just stuffed the food into his mouth, three or four chips at a time, followed by a chilli. James watched as the man chewed with his mouth open.

*How gross!*

After eating, James was keen to get back to work on the wall. He wondered what the man had planned. Not knowing was the worst part. James looked up and stared. The man stared back, their eyes locking together. Once again James was first to look away. Gerard smiled.

*Still my rules kid.*

Now that he'd eaten, Gerard's mind was back on what he would do with the girl.

"You brats finished?" Gerard asked. Both had stopped eating. When he received no answer, he wrapped up the remaining chips in the paper and threw it into the rubbish, put the chilli jar back in the cupboard, locked the door, and went out front to see if the dog walkers had returned.

When he looked out of the office window, he noticed their car was still there. "Patience," he mumbled to himself, before lighting a cigarette, and leaning back against the counter. "You've got all weekend."

**********

"Warner," Robert said, answering the phone on the first ring.

"Hi Robert, there's still no sign of Williamson at the apartment," Watkins said. "But we found the car he stole from the prison parked up at a block of flats in Kilbirnie. What are you up to?"

Warner wasn't about to tell Watkins he'd been ringing real estate agents. "Just tying up a few loose ends. I'm heading off home to Julia shortly," he lied. "Any leads from the car?"

"Forensics is looking at it now. The briefcase was still in the back, but as suspected, Williamson's client file is missing. No more sightings from the public unfortunately. I've talked the *DomPost* into running the updated picture of Williamson in tomorrow morning's paper."

"That should help. Anything else?"

"Not yet. We're still canvassing the Mount Victoria area, but nobody we've spoken to so far remembers seeing him. Williamson could be anywhere by now."

"That's fucking encouraging."

"Look, do you want a sugar-coated version, or do you want my genuine assessment of the situation? This is why you're not involved. Just stay calm and let us do our job."

*Stay calm? My boy's out there in the hands of a madman you dumb fuck!*

**********

As soon as the man closed the door, James reached into his pocket and pulled out the little box containing his mouse, along with a small chip he'd pocketed when the man wasn't looking. He opened the lid, and dropped the chip into the box thinking the mouse might want some food. The mouse wasn't looking very well, but James didn't have time to think about that now. He closed the box and put it back in his pocket.

James walked over to the sink and opened the cupboard. "Okay Ashna, you listen. I'm going to start digging again."

"Before you do," she said. "I've been thinking and I've got an idea."

Ashna's serious tone made James stop. He sat back down beside her, eager to hear what she had to say.

After outlining her plan, Ashna told him what her brother had said the previous night about the man who'd escaped from prison, what he'd done, and how she was sure their captor must be the same person. It only took Ashna a couple of minutes to lay it all out. Afterwards, James asked her a few questions. Ashna answered them as best she could.

Ashna's plan sounded good. James thought that with the two of them working together it might just work. He threw in a suggestion of his own, and after a brief discussion, they decided to give it a go. The plan was daring and they'd need a bit of luck, but it wasn't like they had many options. Dismantling the wall might take too long, and if what Ashna suspected about the man was true, their time could be running out. The plan had to work. The alternative was too scary for words.

"Okay Ashna, I'll grab that brick. You keep listening."

**********

The two detectives arrived at the next site on their list and followed the same routine as last time. They parked well past the warehouse unit and walked cautiously back. This building was steel-framed, and covered with corrugated iron siding. A roller door with a smaller access door in it filled most of its front.

"So what now?" Andy asked.

"Let's just see if we can get a peek inside."

They crept along the exterior of the building and stopped beside the small door inset into the larger roller door. There was a narrow gap where the locking mechanism joined the main frame of the door.

Chris watched as Andy bent down and peered through the crack.

"Bugger, this place is empty too."

**********

While the man was away, James and Ashna took the remaining crepe bandage from the first aid kit and, with the one in James's pocket, twisted them into a thin cord. Once woven together the bandages seemed quite strong. James gave their handmade rope a quick tug to test it.

Ashna spread dishwashing liquid from the bottle they'd found under the sink thinly, but evenly over the linoleum just inside the doorway where the man normally stood when he first stepped into the room.

**********

As Gerard chopped up two more lines of speed on the counter in the office, he watched through the venetian blinds for the dog walkers to return. Then he noticed a flash of colour coming down the hill. Yes, at last he could see them walking down the path. His heart raced as they came into view. He watched as they loaded the dogs into their car and drove away.

Now the fun could start.

Gerard grabbed the secateurs from a drawer in the workshop and walked slowly toward the room containing his two guests. His hands trembled with excitement.

*This is going to be so good.*

**********

"Now you hold that end and I'll grab this one," James said twisting one end of the bandage around his hand. "Wrap it tight, so it doesn't slip."

Ashna wrapped the bandage twice around her hand before

squeezing it tightly. "I hope he doesn't see it lying across the doorway."

"It's nearly the same colour as the floor. We should be okay." James said. "Remember, when he steps through the door, we both pull the bandage tight and then move towards the sink as hard and fast as we can. The floor is so slippery his feet should slide out from under him."

"Then when he's on the floor, we'll hit him with the bricks," Ashna said.

"Right, and remember to aim for his head. Don't stop until we're absolutely sure he's unconscious."

Ashna heard a noise at the door. "Quiet, here he comes."

"Okay, you ready?" James whispered.

Ashna nodded in reply.

Ashna and James crouched down on either side of the doorway with the bandage stretched across the gap between them along the floor.

Gerard was extremely excited to be starting at last. Holding the secateurs in one hand, he pulled the door back with the other, and stepped into the room.

Before Gerard had the chance to turn his head to see where the kids were, his feet were swept out from under him.

*What the fuck?*

Gerard threw an arm out as he crashed backwards, but it was too late. His tailbone hit the floor with a thud. Then his torso whipped back, and his head cracked onto the linoleum. The contact with the hard floor sent a shockwave up Gerard's spine, and his head felt like someone one had cracked him with a softball bat.

Looking up, all he could see was the blur of James and Ashna advancing on him.

*What's that in your …?*

Gerard found out a split second later when a half-brick split his eyebrow to the bone. Warm blood ran into his eyes.

He threw his arms up, and turned his head to the side, in an attempt to protect himself from the second blow which landed on his temple. James and Ashna kept swinging, pounding at

Gerard's head, arms and neck. Then Gerard saw a flash of light, and everything went black.

"Stop. We don't want to kill him!" James said. "Quick, find something to tie his legs with. I'll start on his hands. Have a look out there for a rope or something."

Ashna and James rolled Gerard onto his stomach. As James started tying Gerard's wrists behind his back with the cord they'd made from the bandages. Ashna walked carefully across the slippery floor into the storage area, her eyes roaming for anything they could use to restrain the man's legs. Seeing a roll of duct tape on the bench, she grabbed it and hurried back into the room, slowing briefly so she didn't slip on the floor.

When Gerard came to he gasped for breath, his head throbbed, and the side of his face and neck felt battered. Blinking hard he tried to clear his vision, but his eyes refused to focus. He attempted to roll onto his back, but couldn't. With his face to the floor, his arms tied firmly behind his back, and his legs bound tightly together, he was helpless.

*What the fuck is going on?*

By twisting his torso and neck, Gerard could see the boy holding the secateurs in one hand, his arm around the girl. They were both smiling down at him.

*Why are they smiling?*

"It's nearly over now Ashna. We'll leave soon," James said.

"Good. I want to go home."

When he looked down at Gerard, James noticed his eyes had opened. "He's awake now, Ashna."

"You sure?"

"Yep, so you go first. Go on, kick him!" James urged Ashna on, his eyes bright and shining.

Ashna kicked Gerard in the ribs as hard as she could. Gerard tried unsuccessfully to squirm away.

"Again Ashna. Kick him again!"

Ashna kicked him again, and again, and once again. Gerard grunted in pain with each blow.

James looked down at the man. "Now, I'm going to teach you a lesson."

Gerard wondered what the boy meant … but only for a moment. A hand grabbed his bound wrists, raising them slightly. Then something sharp clamp onto his little finger.

*What the …?*

When the secateurs cut through bone and tendons, a searing pain flashed up Gerard's arm. He tried to scream, but the tape wrapped around his lower face prevented his mouth from opening. What noise did emerge was more a grunt as the scream burned it way out his nostrils instead. In agony, with jaw clenched and eyes screwed tight, Gerard felt his hands begin to rise once more.

Gerard's ring finger came off with a red hot crunch, followed shortly thereafter by the middle finger. The pain was excruciating. Sweat mixed with blood ran pink down Gerard's forehead. His body shook uncontrollably.

About to pass out, darkness slowly engulfing him, Gerard felt the bite of the steel blades yet again. He gritted his teeth. The only thing keeping him conscious now was terror.

*Fuck, fuck, fuck!*

As Gerard's index finger joined the others in a gathering pool of blood on the floor, the pain was too great to bear, his brain switched off, and darkness took him.

As James looked down at Gerard's inert body he felt an intense ripple of pleasure run through his body.

Cold water thrown onto Gerard's face and head brought him back a few minutes later. When his eyes finally opened Ashna took the secateurs from James and humming her favourite song, went to work on the fingers of Gerard's other hand.

It was not to be Gerard's lucky day after all.

When Ashna had finished, they wiped the blood from their hands onto Gerard's pants. Ashna then wiped off the secateurs and dropped them on the floor next to the inert body of Gerard Williamson.

"Grab a towel and let's clean our fingerprints off anything we've touched," James instructed. "It's important we do it properly."

As usual, Ashna obeyed James's instructions.

Once their cleanup was finished, James led Ashna from the room, closing the door on their way out.

"Now you remember the story we're going to tell the cops eh?" James said, smiling. "The guy kept us locked in his van for a while, and then dropped us off on the main road. We don't know where he's gone."

"What if they find him?" Ashna asked.

"Somebody's bound to find him eventually, but by then he won't be talking."

Pulling the small box out of his pocket, James opened its lid and looked down at the mouse inside. It still had two pins sticking out of its small brown body, one from James, the other inserted by Ashna. James poked the mouse a few times with his finger, but it was dead. He showed it to Ashna, smiled, then closed the box and dropped it into the crate under the bench as they passed.

They both felt so damn good.

It was getting dark as Ashna and James walked out of the building and down to the end of the street. Turning left onto the main road, they headed toward the lights of Lower Hutt. They'd ring home once they were well away from this place.

As Chris and Andy drove back towards Wellington after checking the last of the warehouses on their list, they saw two children walking hand in hand down the street towards Lower Hutt.

As they drew closer Andy said, "I can't believe it. There they are!"

"Well I'll be buggered." Chris replied. "It looks like this case is going to have a happy ending after all."

********

# More from Blair Polly

*Art, Sharks, and a Coffin Named Denzel*

Alex is a sculptor with big dreams and an over-active imagination. When he meets the gorgeous Lisa he can't believe his luck, but Lisa has a secret that threatens not only her budding relationship with Alex, but the lives of Alex's friends as well.

*Art, Sharks and a Coffin Named Denzel* gives a humorous insight into the workings of a creative mind. It is also a story of friendship, love, courage, and how valuable time becomes when it's about to run out.

A suspenseful and emotional roller-coaster with an ending you won't expect.

"A quirky, suspenseful, and funny read."

"I enjoyed the characters, many of whom felt like close friends by the end of the book."

# MORE FROM BLAIR POLLY

*Above High Tide*

Investigator, Sam McKee, would rather enjoy himself fossicking for jade and artefacts on the rugged West Coast of New Zealand's South Island, than worry about the stranger he's seen digging a grave on the river flats and staring at a young girl in the local village.

Lydia would rather be living with someone other than Mr G, but she doesn't have a safe exit strategy and Mr G isn't the sort of man a girl says no to.

Mr G wants it all. His brothels make him plenty of money, but that's not enough. His property empire, held together with blackmail and extortion, is under threat, and he will do whatever it takes to keep it.

Sam will need all his skills as an investigator, diplomat, and gambler if he's to satisfy a violent egomaniac, especially one who's out for blood. Can he save the life of someone who's just made a stupid mistake without risking his own? Or will he end up buried *Above High Tide*?

* * *

For updates and more, check out Blair Polly's website:
www.blairpolly.com

Or email Blair at: bpolly@xtra.co.nz

3158858R00104

Printed in Germany
by Amazon Distribution
GmbH, Leipzig